Transfixed, Russ stared at the child in Laura's arms.

"My name is James Russell Ramirez," the boy suddenly said.

If there were any lingering doubts in Russ's mind, the announcement dispelled them. This was his son, and Laura had kept his existence a secret for six years. "Why didn't you tell me?" Russ asked Laura.

After coaxing her son into his bedroom, she answered. "Why should I have told you? Would you have asked me to marry you?"

Russ let his arms fall to his sides. He hadn't been interested in settling down back then—with anyone. It was only after he'd lost her that he realized how much she'd meant to him.

"Who knows, Russ? There might be a chance for some sort of relationship even at this late date."

Was she referring to herself as well as their son?

Dear Reader,

In celebration of Valentine's Day, we have a Special Edition lineup filled with love and romance!

Cupid reignites passion between two former lovebirds in this month's THAT'S MY BABY! title. *Valentine Baby* by Gina Wilkins is about a fallen firefighter who returns home on Valentine's Day to find a baby—and his former sweetheart offering a shocking marriage proposal!

Since so many of you adored Silhouette's MONTANA MAVERICKS series, we have a special treat in store for you over the next few months in Special Edition. Jackie Merritt launches the MONTANA MAVERICKS: RETURN TO WHITEHORN series with a memorable story about a lovelorn cowboy and the woman who makes his life complete, in *Letter to a Lonesome Cowboy.* And coming up are three more books in the series as well as a delightful collection of short stories and an enthralling Harlequin Historical title.

These next three books showcase how children can bond people together in the most miraculous ways. In *Wildcatter's Kid,* by Penny Richards, a young lad reunites his parents. This is the final installment of the SWITCHED AT BIRTH miniseries. Next, *Natural Born Trouble,* by veteran author Sherryl Woods—the second book in her AND BABY MAKES THREE: THE NEXT GENERATION miniseries—is an uplifting story about a reserved heroine who falls for the charms of rambunctious twin boys...and their sexy father! And a sweet seven-year-old inspires a former rebel to reclaim his family, in *Daddy's Home,* by Pat Warren.

Finally, Celeste Hamilton unfolds an endearing tale about two childhood pals who make all their romantic dreams come true, in *Honeymoon Ranch.*

I hope you enjoy this book and each and every title to come!

Sincerely,

Tara Gavin,
Senior Editor and Editorial Coordinator

Please address questions and book requests to:
Silhouette Reader Service
U.S.: 3010 Walden Ave., P.O. Box 1325, Buffalo, NY 14269
Canadian: P.O. Box 609, Fort Erie, Ont. L2A 5X3

PENNY RICHARDS
WILDCATTER'S KID

SPECIAL EDITION®

Published by Silhouette Books

America's Publisher of Contemporary Romance

This book is for Tara, who came up with a great and fun
idea. Thanks. For Zachery, my dark-haired, blue-eyed,
soon-to-be-a-heartthrob grandson, for lending me his
name. Love you, Zach! And for Suzannah—good friend,
writing partner, travelin' buddy. I miss you.

Special thanks to Karen Taylor Richman for her keen eye
and keeping "all our ducks in a row."

SILHOUETTE BOOKS

ISBN 0-373-24155-0

WILDCATTER'S KID

Books by Penny Richards

Silhouette Special Edition

The Greatest Gift of All #921
Where Dreams Have Been #949
Sisters #1015
*The Ranger and the Schoolmarm #1136
*Wildcatter's Kid #1155

*Switched at Birth

Previously published under the pseudonym Bay Matthews

Silhouette Special Editon

Bittersweet Sacrifice #298
Roses and Regrets #347
Some Warm Hunger #391
Lessons in Loving #420
Amarillo by Morning #464
Summer's Promise #505
Laughter on the Wind #613
Sweet Lies, Satin Sighs #648
Worth Waiting For #825
Hardhearted #859

Silhouette Books

Silhouette Christmas Stories 1989
"A Christmas Carole"

PENNY RICHARDS,

of Haughton, Louisiana, describes herself as a dreamer and an incurable romantic. Married at an early age to her high school sweetheart, she claims she grew up with her three children. Now that only the youngest is at home, writing romances adds an exciting new dimension to her life.

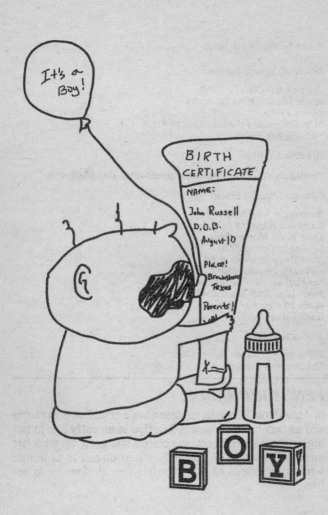

Chapter One

Laura Ramirez blew out a nervous breath and pressed the doorbell. A musical chiming sounded from somewhere inside Zach and Georgia Rawlings's new home. Laura rocked up and down on her toes. Though the wait seemed endless, the door swung open in a matter of seconds.

"Hey there, gorgeous!" Zach said, giving her a brief hug. Laura was tempted to throw her arms around her friend's neck and bawl the way Rufio had when she'd left him with her sister. Instead, she pulled free and gave Zach a weak smile.

"Thanks for having me over on such short notice."

"No problem." Zach led the way inside and indicated a wing chair. "Have a seat." When she complied, he asked, "What's up?"

"I've found out something that throws a whole new light on the night you and Jake were born," she told him, knowing the information she was about to give him wasn't what he expected her to find when he asked her to check into why he and his twin were separated at birth.

She'd already found out why Abby Rawlings had given Jake up, a question that had plagued Zach and his twin brother, Jake Lattimer, since late May when Georgia, Zach's new wife, had seen him at the airport and mistaken him for Jake—whom she'd been engaged to at the time.

When Zach, a Texas Ranger working on a sting at the airport, took a hit on the head during the arrest attempt, Georgia had refused to believe the law officers who told her he wasn't Jake. She insisted on accompanying him to the hospital, where she admitted him under her fiancé's name.

When Zach had awakened with temporary amnesia, Georgia had done the only thing she could. She'd driven him home—to the Lazy L Ranch—filling him in on the missing pieces of his life during the trip. It had come as a tremendous shock when she'd pulled up in front of the house and the real Jake came bursting out the door.

Their unmistakable resemblance had raised dozens of questions no one could answer. Ben Lattimer, Jake's dad, had sorrowfully confessed that Jake had been adopted by him and his deceased wife, Retha. As stunned as both younger men, he swore that he had no knowledge of any other child.

Jake had been devastated. Zach, with no memory, was even more confused.

Ben had pushed for DNA tests, and the results had been positive. Jake and Zach were undeniably brothers. No one involved had any knowledge of how such a thing as separating the two could have happened—not senatorial candidate Tom Barnette, who'd handled the adoption for the Lattimers, or Lillian Hampstead, the aging, senile nurse who remembered little of the stormy night Jake was born.

When Zach's memory returned a couple of weeks later, he added a whole new wrinkle to the dilemma. He was completely convinced that the woman who raised him was his birth mother, not someone who'd adopted him. His dad, Dwayne Rawlings, had confirmed that yes, indeedy, Abby Pickett Rawlings had given him birth. When Zach asked why she'd given away his twin brother, Jake, a stunned Dwayne had dropped another bombshell. He knew nothing about any twins because he wasn't Zach's biological father. Zach was two months old when he'd started seeing Abby Pickett, and five months old when they'd married.

The new questions plaguing everyone became why Abby had given away one of her babies, and who had fathered them. Zach had come to Laura, who was already working on a piece about the changes in adoption policies for the *Dallas Morning News,* hoping she could help ferret out the truth.

After several dead-end interviews Laura had begun to believe there was some sort of cover-up, but finally, a few days ago, she'd received a tidbit of information she felt was the truth about what had happened, which solved at least part of the puzzle to her satisfaction.

"I have a theory about what happened that night," she told Zach, "but it's only speculation at this point." She glanced around. "Where's Georgia?"

"She's making a pot of coffee," Zach said. He

grinned, the smile so like his brother's. "You've really got my curiosity up."

"About what?" Georgia Rawlings asked from the doorway.

Zach patted the spot on the sofa next to him. "Laura's found out something about the night Jake and I were born."

Laura shifted in her chair. "I haven't found out anything...exactly. It's more of a very strong hunch."

"Well, whatever it is, spit it out."

"Okay." Laura looked from Georgia to Zach and back again. "I have reason to believe you and Jake were switched with the Campbell twins at the hospital the night you were born."

Laura had always heard the saying "so quiet you could hear a pin drop," but she'd never experienced it until that moment.

"How on earth would you come up with a cockamamie idea like that?" Zach asked, finally breaking the silence.

"I spoke with Valerie Campbell a few days ago," Laura told him. "She didn't remember much about that night, but she did tell me that her *twin* sons were born the same night as you and Jake."

"Logan and Russ Campbell are twins?" Zach asked, the news as much a shock to him as it had been to Laura.

She nodded. "Fraternal. I knew they were near the same age, but I assumed they were born a year apart or something. Finding out they're twins was a shock. I can't believe Ben or Jake or *someone* didn't tell me."

"I didn't know," Zach said.

"Jake told me the Campbells were twins several

years ago, but I never thought to tell you," Georgia said. "They don't look anything alike, and they've lived such separate lives, I never think of them as twins. I don't think anyone else does, either."

"I don't get it," Zach said, having thought about it for a moment. "Why would hearing that Logan and Russ—twins—were born the same night as Jake and I give you the idea that we were switched?"

Laura looked from one expectant face to the other. They were fast approaching the hard part.

"Do you remember me saying that Lillian Hampstead told me your mother gave away one of her babies because it had a heart condition and she couldn't handle the burden of the medical bills?"

"Yeah," Zach said, nodding. "We figured that's why she chose to keep me and let Jake go with the Lattimers."

"Right. We were all walking around scratching our heads over that one, since it turned out neither you nor Jake has a history of heart problems. If I'd known Logan and Russ were twins I'd probably have considered accidental switching as a possibility much sooner."

"What makes you so sure you're right?" Zach asked.

Laura took a deep breath and plunged. "Abby supposedly gave away one of her babies because it had a heart problem, but neither you nor Jake has one. Okay. Valerie told me Jack was anxious to be on the way after her babies were born, so they checked out of the hospital the next day. A few days later, after they got settled, she found a doctor so she could make sure you two were okay. That's when they found out Russ had a small hole in his heart."

"What?"

"You're kidding!"

Georgia and Zach spoke in unison. Laura nodded.

No one spoke for a moment. Laura watched her friend's face while he worked through the information she'd given him.

"If it was as wild that night as everyone says it was—no phones, no doctor, three women in labor, it isn't so farfetched," she said. "I'd guess it's fairly unusual for any hospital to have two sets of twins born the same night, especially one as small as Brownsboro General."

"Nurse Hampstead must have mixed you up in all the confusion," Georgia said. She looked at her husband. "It makes sense, Zach."

He rubbed his mustache with his forefinger. "I guess it's possible," he said grudgingly.

Georgia reached for her husband's hand, a sudden look of alarm on her pixie face. "Oh, gosh, Zach. If it's true—and it must be—it means that Abby wasn't your mother, after all."

The shock in Zach's eyes told Laura he hadn't thought that far ahead. "Are you saying Jake and I are Jack and Valerie Campbell's?"

Laura nodded. "That's exactly what I'm saying."

Zach leaped to his feet and went to the window. Georgia looked at Laura as if to ask what she should do. Laura gave a helpless shrug. She could only imagine what Zach must be feeling. To find out that the woman who'd raised you as her own, the woman who had nursed you from her breasts, wasn't your mother at all, must be a staggering revelation.

"When you think about it," Laura said, "it makes sense. Russ played baseball as a kid, and Logan plays tennis. Jack played football, and both you and Jake were football players in high school.''

''Not to mention that you and Jake look a lot more like Jack and Valerie than you do the pictures I've seen of Abby,'' Georgia said, then added, ''Oh, my gosh! That's why neither Logan's nor Russ's blood type was compatible to Jack's when they were looking for donors before Jack's surgery.''

''Right,'' Laura said.

Zach looked dazed. ''I remember Mom saying Grandpa Pickett had red hair,'' he said, turning from the window to face them. ''Logan's hair is sandy colored, and Russ's is auburn.'' He looked from one woman to the other. ''I guess that about tears it. Have you told Jake?''

Laura shook her head. ''You were the one who wanted me to check into things, so I wanted to tell you first.''

''What about Logan and Russ? Do they know?''

Laura shook her head. ''If you like, I can go to New Orleans with you when you and Jake break the news to...Logan.''

Zach swore. ''It'll tear them up to find out they aren't Black Jack Campbell's boys.''

''No more than it has you to find out Abby Pickett wasn't your mother,'' Georgia said. ''No more than it will Jake. At least the two of you finally know the truth. If anyone has any doubts, you can always have more DNA tests, right, Laura?''

Tests. Rufio...her little boy's tests. Proof of his heart condition...

''Laura?'' Georgia said. ''Are you okay? You look a little queasy.''

''I'm fine,'' she said, attempting a smile.

"Are you sure?"

"Yeah."

Russ's look was speculative. "What aren't you telling us?"

"Nothing."

"Come on, *chica*. I know you better than that," Zach said. "The jig's up. If you don't come clean, I'll have to tickle you until you tell."

Despite her anxiety, Laura laughed. Zach was one of the few people who knew how ticklish she was. He was also one of the few people she could trust with her secret. A secret that would soon be general knowledge.

"It isn't about the adoptions...except maybe in an indirect way." She leaned against the sofa cushions and clasped her hands together on her crossed knees. "I'm about to tell you something that can go no further than the two of you, Ben, Jake and...and Logan. At least not for a few days."

"Don't tell me there's another skeleton in the closet."

"Not yours. Mine." Laura forced her gaze to Zach's. "I know you've always been curious about J.R's father."

Zach nodded, his grin sardonic. "The little brat's paternity has crossed my mind from time to time. The name Beelzebub came to mind once or twice."

"Very funny," Laura said, with a halfhearted smile at his attempted humor. "I didn't tell anyone because the man didn't show any sign of wanting a permanent relationship. I thought the best thing to do was keep my mouth shut, raise my baby as best I could and get on with my life."

She felt the hot scald of tears. "Because of J.R.'s

heart condition, I need a complete family medical history. I'm forced to tell his father about him."

"*Chica*...c'mon, darlin', don't cry," Zach pleaded. "You don't have to tell me anything you don't want to. We'll love the little ankle biter no matter who his father is."

Zach's comment brought a brief, teary laugh, just as she knew he'd hoped it would.

"I may as well tell you now, because everyone will know soon." She met Zach's gaze squarely. "Russ is Rufio's father."

"Russ?" Georgia echoed. "Russ *Campbell?*"

Laura nodded miserably. "That's what made me so sure you were switched. When I talked to Valerie, I found out for the first time that Logan and Russ were twins. I'd just found out about J.R.'s heart problem. Russ had heart problems as a child. Abby gave away a baby with heart problems. It fits, folks. As tight as a new leather glove."

"Russ Campbell is your little boy's father?" Jake asked later that afternoon when Laura joined Zach and Georgia at the Lazy L. Jake seemed more discombobulated by that bit of news than he was to hear Laura's theory about him and Zach being switched with Logan and Russ.

"Turn up your hearing aid, cowboy," Jake's new wife, Shelby, said in a sardonic voice. "That's what the lady said." To Laura, whom she'd known for several years, she added, "You sure know how to keep a secret, girl."

When Jake still didn't say anything, Zach said, "Well, what do you think, hoss?"

Jake shrugged. "After all we've been through since

Georgia dragged your ratty butt home from the hospital and I found out Retha wasn't my real mom and Ben isn't my real dad, hearing that Jack Campbell *is* doesn't seem like such a big deal.''

''Just another day at the ranch,'' Shelby drawled.

''Right,'' Jake agreed. ''Knowing Jack was my dad is better than not knowing who my old man was.'' He looked at Zach and grinned. ''No offense, but Jack beats heck out of Dwayne Rawlings.''

''No kidding,'' Zach said.

Jake smiled sadly. ''I was sort of getting used to the idea of Abby being my mom, though. I hate to lose her.''

The lost expression Zach had worn the week or so he'd had amnesia and had no idea who he was made a brief appearance in his dark eyes. ''Yeah.''

''You'll like Valerie,'' Jake said. ''She's a great lady. Dad and I have always been really fond of her.'' He scrubbed a hand down his face. ''I can't believe it. Valerie Campbell is my mother. It's crazy.''

''It's crazy,'' Jake said to Shelby that night as they lay side by side in their king-size bed. ''I've had three mothers since last May. Retha, Abby and now Valerie.''

Shelby raised herself on one elbow and looked at him in the moonlit darkness. While she understood the natural confusion he'd gone through the past few months, Shelby, a former cop for the Dallas Police Department who'd been shuffled from one foster home to another as a kid, couldn't dredge up much sympathy. ''You're kind of special, then, aren't you?''

Jake laughed. Shelby had a way of making his worries seem groundless. "Yeah," he said, "I guess I am." He pulled her down and kissed her softly. "That's what I love about you, Shel. You never let me feel sorry for myself, and you always make me look at things from a different perspective."

"I learned that being a cop," she said.

"Really?"

"Yeah. You always look at things from every possible angle, so you're less likely to make some stupid mistake or overlook something important."

"It's a good way to approach life."

"I think so." She put her hand against his cheek. "You're all right with this, aren't you? I mean, I know you like Val a lot. We all do. It can't be too hard to accept that she's the person who gave birth to you, can it?"

He shook his head. "It won't be as hard for me as it will be for Zach." He smiled. "She and I always got along. Jack and I did, too. I remember him throwing the football to me when I was a kid and he'd come over to take care of some sort of business with Dad."

"It's good you have some memories," Shelby said. "Be thankful you had a chance to get to know him before he died and that there's still time for you and Valerie to have a relationship."

"I am thankful," Jake said.

"And while you're counting your blessings, I have another one."

"What's that, sugar?" Jake asked.

Shelby touched her lips to his. He could feel her smiling against his mouth. "We're gonna have a baby."

* * *

Georgia Rawlings awakened from a sound sleep and found the place next to her empty. Looking toward the French doors that led to the patio outside their bedroom, she saw Zach's silhouette outlined against the shimmering light of the moon.

She threw back the sheet and padded across the room. She opened the door softly, slipped outside and put her arms around his hard middle, savoring the scent of his skin, cherishing the knowledge that he was hers.

"Are you all right?" she asked, her hand brushing the open waistband of the jeans he'd put on before going outside.

"Yeah. I guess," he said over his shoulder. He carried her hand to his lips. "Sorry I woke you."

"You didn't." She nuzzled his back with her lips. "Do you want to talk about it?"

"Not really." Then, in direct contradiction to the denial, he said, "It's hard to believe, even with all the evidence."

"You can always have more DNA tests to prove it."

"We probably will, but I don't need tests to prove what my gut is telling me is true." He turned and pulled her against him. "How could such a thing happen, sunshine?"

"How can any bad thing happen, Zach? It just does. Sometimes it's deliberate, but just as often, it's an accident…a careless mistake."

"Well, it's a heck of a thing to have so many lives torn apart because of a careless mistake."

"I know."

Zach was quiet for several moments. "Abby was a good mother," he said at last. "And a fine person.

I'm sorry Logan and Russ won't have the opportunity to get to know her.''

"So am I. But look on the good side. You've found a brother you didn't know you had, a brother you're building a strong relationship with. Ben has done everything but take out adoption papers on you,'' she said with a soft gurgle of laughter, "so you finally have a father who cares about you. And you're going to have the chance to get to know your real mother.''

Zach didn't reply. "It could be a lot worse,'' she said. "Think about Logan and Russ. If Laura can't find out who their biological father is, they'll never have the chance to get to know either of their real parents.''

"That's the craziest thing I ever heard,'' Logan Campbell said the next day.

Jake had flown himself, Zach and Laura from Texas to New Orleans in the Lazy L helicopter after they'd explained Laura's theory to Ben. Logan had agreed to meet them at the Gaspard Building, which was quiet on a Friday afternoon after business hours. At Laura's request, Russ, who was working out of town, wasn't encouraged to attend the meeting. She could only handle one crisis at a time.

Starting at the beginning, they detailed everything that had happened over the past few weeks—Jake telling Logan about Georgia bringing Zach to the Lazy L, Zach explaining how he'd brought Laura into the picture when he got back his memory and wanted to find out the truth about his father, Laura recounting her meetings with Lillian Hampstead and Tom Barnette and explaining how the information she'd gleaned from her talk with Valerie made all the pieces fall into place.

Even so, Logan was having a hard time buying it.

"And if it *is* true," he went on, as he paced from one side of the elegantly appointed office to the other, "you can bet the Lazy L that if Barnette was involved in *any* way, there was more to it than meets the eye."

"Are you still on your Barnette vendetta?" Jake asked. "I thought you'd given up on that since you're trying to get your schedule whittled down to take a honeymoon at Christmas."

"I have...more or less," Logan said. "But just because I've turned in all the information I have to the attorney general's office doesn't mean my opinion of the man has changed. He's slime. Always was. Always will be."

"You won't get any argument out of me," Jake said. He looked at his friend with compassion. "Believe me. Zach and I know what a shock this must be to you—we've already been through a couple of varying scenarios ourselves—but I think it's a little prejudicial to assume there was anything nefarious going on just because Barnette was involved in my adoption. Obviously, it was an innocent mistake."

"Maybe," Logan admitted in a grudging voice. He shoved a hand through his hair, a familiar gesture he shared with his brother. "Jeez, Russ is going to go ballistic when we tell him." He cast a curious look at Jake and Zach. "Why didn't you want him here this afternoon? He's coming in for the weekend. I could have asked him to make it a day early."

Instead of answering, Zach looked at Laura. "Truth or dare, hot stuff."

Laura turned to the older Campbell, who, in his

youth, had been dubbed Golden Boy by the press. The name fit. Logan Campbell exuded success from the top of his well-groomed, sandy head to the tips of his hand-crafted Italian loafers. He was so totally unlike his rough and ready brother, it was little wonder no one suspected they were twins. In fact, they were so dissimilar in looks and attitude that if she didn't know better, she might not even believe they were brothers.

She reached into her purse and drew a wallet-size picture from a plastic sleeve. Without speaking, she got up, crossed the room and handed the photo to Logan.

His eyebrows snapped together. "Where'd you get this picture of Russ?"

"It isn't Russ," Laura said. "But his name *is* James Russell Ramirez. He's my son. And Russ's."

Instead of the explosion she expected, Logan raised a bleak gaze to hers, unable to deny what was so clear.

"J.R.—I call him that because he's so ornery—he's five, and he…" Her voice trailed away as she paused to try to control its sudden quaver. "He was just diagnosed with a heart problem."

Logan stared at her. If anything, this bit of news was as shocking as hearing that he and Russ weren't Jack Campbell's boys.

"Is he going to be all right?"

Laura nodded. "His condition can be controlled with medication, and there's a chance he'll outgrow it."

"Damn Russ! He never said a word to any of us about having a child."

"He didn't know," Laura said. "But the doctors

want a complete medical history, so I have to tell him now."

"Why didn't you say anything before?"

She gave a dismissive lift of her shoulders. "I met Russ six years ago when I covered the Odessa blowout. He made it clear that he didn't want a commitment, and I wouldn't settle for anything less. So, when I found out I was pregnant, it seemed best for everyone that I just keep quiet. I was afraid that if I told him about the baby, he'd marry me out of a sense of duty. You know how Russ is."

"Yeah. Selfish and self-centered."

"If you think that, then you don't know your brother very well," Laura said. "He's an adventurer, a free spirit. If he'd lived a hundred years ago, he'd have been a pirate or an explorer. He wasn't meant to be bound by anyone or anything. Laying a guilt trip on him and forcing him to face his responsibilities wouldn't have been good for any of us. Especially J.R."

Logan digested that for a moment, then said, "So you're going to tell him?"

"I'll tell Russ the truth. But in my own way, my own time. I need to tell J.R. about his dad and let him get used to the idea of having one before they meet."

"Should I tell Russ about this mix-up you've uncovered?" Logan asked.

Laura nodded. "You and Jake and Zach can break the news to Russ and Valerie. I don't mind if you tell Russ it came out during an investigation Zach requested, but I'd appreciate your not mentioning me or J.R. just yet."

Logan nodded. "I'll talk to Mom this evening.

Russ is due back in town some time tonight. I'll give him a call first thing in the morning."

Laura stood and picked up her purse. "Good. I'll catch a flight to Dallas and start working things from my end." She reached for the photo.

"Do you mind if I keep this?" Logan asked, staring at the snapshot. "I'd sort of like of have a picture of my only nephew."

"Sure," Laura said, touched by the gesture. "I'm sorry to have been the one to break such bad news to you."

"Actually, I feel a little numb. I don't think it's really soaked in, yet."

"The worse is yet to come," Jake said in an oblique reference to the upcoming meeting with Russ.

Logan shook his head. "You can say that again. Russ never has been much for changing up the status quo."

Russ Campbell leaned against the bar, nursing a stiff Scotch on the rocks and watching couples surrounded by cigarette smoke swaying to a Whitney Houston ballad on the minuscule dance floor. One couple—who was all but making love with their clothes on—hadn't moved a foot since the song began.

As he watched the man and woman rubbing against each other, two things became crystal clear. He was well on his way to being three sheets to the wind, and he was as lonely as hell. His dad's death had left a void in his life no amount of work had been able to fill. The abyss had grown larger when his brother and Bliss Abernathy, the woman who'd been brought up as his sister, had decided to get married and she moved out of the small camping trailer they'd called home for the past six years and into the Gaspard mansion with his mother.

Yep, he thought, lifting the glass, he was downright lonesome. Not just for his dad, but for feminine companionship. Logan and Bliss's happiness after finally resolving their lifelong differences only sharpened Russ's growing dissatisfaction.

Truth was, Baby Sister Bliss wasn't the only one in the Campbell clan ready for a change. He still liked the oil business, still liked being outdoors, but more and more lately, he felt as if he were missing something.

Yeah, Campbell. Like sex.

He drained his glass and plunked it down with a curt order for another to the college type mixing drinks behind the lustrous mahogany bar.

It had been a long time since he'd had a woman, and that was part of the problem. But despite the rampant rumors about his sexual prowess, he wasn't a bed hopper, and the older he got, the less inclined he felt to put forth the effort it took to forge and maintain a long-term relationship.

He didn't know what was wrong with him, but he didn't like it, and tonight, he refused to dwell on it. The bartender pushed a full glass toward him, and Russ—never one for more than a couple of beers—grabbed it gratefully, knowing he'd be sorry in the morning.

He wouldn't think about that, either. Maybe he'd ask that pretty Latino girl to dance, instead. He liked her petite, lush body, the way her eyes flashed when she laughed and the way she tossed her dark, curly hair.

Uh-uh. Don't go there, laddie. It'll just make you more miserable.

The wee voice inside his head was right, but sometimes he had to take out the memories of the time he'd spent with Laura Ramirez and look at them no matter how much grief they caused.

Not tonight.

No. Not tonight. Tonight he was going to forget everything—his dad's death, the fact that Bliss, his best friend, was forsaking him for marriage, and the relentless memories of six of the most satisfying and memorable weeks of his life…time he'd spent with Laura. And if it took getting stinking drunk to do it, then by golly, that's what he'd do.

An hour later, it could be said that Russ had accomplished his mission. He'd laughed, danced and flirted with the pretty *señorita*, whose name was Felicity. He'd downed enough Scotch to drown a fairsize dog. He was feeling fine. He'd have just one more drink, he thought, beaming at the crowded room, and then he'd feel Felicity up—oops! Uh, he'd feel her *out*—about continuing their budding acquaintance.

"I think you've had enough, buddy," the bartender said, swooping Russ's glass off the bar and banishing it to the land of dirty glassware.

Russ straightened on the bar stool. "And I think you'd better reconsider."

The bartender might have been young, but he knew his business. He didn't even bother answering. He just looked across the room, gave a jerk of his chin and went on wiping down the bar.

In seconds, Russ felt a heavy arm fall across his shoulders. He turned. The guy—the bouncer, no doubt—could have been a first cousin to King Kong. His bristly face looked as if it had been used for Evander Holyfield's punching bag.

"How you feelin', dude?" the ape man asked with a friendly smile.

"I feel fine," Russ said, grinning. "Primo, in fact."

"That so?" Kong said. "Well, you look a little peaked to me. Maybe you ought to go outside and get a little fresh air."

Russ squinted at him. "Y'think so?"

"Definitely. Better yet, why don't I call you a cab?"

Russ shrugged and grinned. "Okay." He stood with the man's help. "Jus' a minute. I want to ask my frien' something."

"Sure thing, buddy."

"Hey, Felicity!" he yelled. "I'm goin' home now. Wanna marry me?"

Felicity turned her back on him, and Kong grabbed Russ's shirt and dragged him out the door. The humid air hit him like a smack in the face. The bouncer propped him against the side of the building, asked his address and went inside to call a cab.

Russ was watching the traffic go by and humming the Whitney Houston song when Felicity sidled up to him. What happened next was a blur. She said something to him, pulled his face down for a sizzling kiss and rubbed up against him like a cat in heat. The next thing Russ knew, he was being hauled around by some goon only slightly smaller than his new buddy, the bouncer.

The first blow took Russ by surprise. The second went a long way toward clearing his head. By the third, he was sober enough to realize he was in a world of trouble. He gathered what he could of his soused wits and struck back, landing a solid blow to his assailant's midsection. He hadn't been in a good fistfight in years, but it felt so good, so *right* when he hit the guy that he wondered why he'd given brawling up.

He wasn't sure how long he exchanged blows with the stranger, but by the time the door opened and Kong yelled a blistering curse, Russ thought he was getting the upper hand. Hearing the bouncer's angry curse, the stranger took off, Felicity in tow.

"You okay?" Kong asked, steadying Russ as the taxi pulled to the curb.

"Fine," Russ said, feeling anything but. His euphoria and a large percentage of his drunkenness had evaporated during the assault. He was already thinking ahead to the next day and the repercussions of his night of debauchery.

Kong laughed. "You're gonna have a shiner tomorrow."

"Yeah, well, you ought to see the other guy," Russ said testily, still wondering what had happened.

"I did." Kong grinned. "Looked like his face had been through a tenderizer. I'll bet he didn't expect you to put up such a fight or he'd have picked someone else to mug."

"Mug?"

Kong nodded. "I try to watch out for women like that. I can usually spot them a mile away, but it's been a busy night."

He helped Russ inside the taxi, gave the cabbie the address and tapped the top of the car a couple of times. As the car pulled away from the curb, he shouted, "Take care of that eye, dude!"

The sound of jangling bells inside his head roused Russ from a deep sleep. He squeezed his eyes shut and willed the noise, which he realized was the telephone, to stop. When it didn't, he rolled over and flung out his arm. His hand connected with hair. His touch elicited a contented sigh, and Russ froze, the ringing phone forgotten.

Dear sweet heaven! Had he picked up some woman? He bolted upright—his first mistake of the day—and saw to his relief that it wasn't a strange woman in his bed. It was only his mutt, Gusher, who'd taken to sleeping with him since Bliss abandoned them for Logan and big-city life.

When the phone rang again, Russ snatched it from its base with a snarled hello.

"A little testy this morning, are we?"

Russ recognized his brother's sardonic voice. "What the hell do you want?" he growled.

Logan chuckled. "Rough night?"

Russ grabbed his head. "Argh!" he said. "Don't talk so loud."

Logan's answer was another laugh. "Get your sorry carcass up, take a couple of aspirin and come down to the Gaspard Building. I need to talk to you about something."

Russ opened his mouth to ask what was so all-fired important that Logan had to wake him at six in the morning and heard a sudden buzzing in his ear. He stared at the receiver, his mouth hanging open in surprise.

Logan had hung up on him.

Chapter Two

Minutes before the appointed time, his jaw clenched, trendy Ray-Bans shielding his bloodshot, amber-tinted eyes, Russ shoved his way through the double doors of the Gaspard Building, a five-story edifice just off Canal Street. Built in 1896, the red brick structure housed the offices of Gaspard Enterprises, whose various business interests were managed by Logan, and to a lesser degree, their mother.

Russ sported a black eye and a purpling bruise on his left jaw. His body felt as if it had been used for a punching bag, and his head pounded with every step of his Nike Airs.

He was hung over and hungry, a combination he'd learned was lethal to anyone who crossed him—which is exactly what Logan had done by phoning him so dad-burned early on a Saturday morning.

The events of the night before were still somewhat

hazy. He remembered arriving in New Orleans from the newest Campbell Drilling site in south Texas and stopping at a bar, where he'd succumbed to two evils he'd managed to escape since his aborted, three-month stint at college almost seventeen years before—he'd gotten thoroughly, stinkingly drunk and had gotten into a fight. Thus, the sore jaw, pounding head and multiplicity of bruises.

In the aftermath, he realized that neither diversion was any more satisfying at thirty-five than it had been at eighteen. Heck, he couldn't even remember what had triggered the brawl, but he was thankful no one had called the cops. If his dad were still alive he'd have skinned Russ alive for "sullying the Campbell name" and "making a damned fool of himself in a public place." Besides that, Jack Campbell had refused to have anyone who drank more than the occasional beer working on his rigs since his best friend, Chuck Abernathy, had died in a drilling accident and left his daughter, Bliss, for Jack to raise.

But Jack wasn't there, and that, Russ knew, was the real reason he'd gotten drunk. Black Jack Campbell had died just over three weeks ago. The heart attack that ended his life had shaken Russ, reminding him of the congenital heart condition that made his early years torment.

But it was more than recognition of his mortality that had his emotions in turmoil. It was losing his best friend and most constant companion. The pain of Jack's passing was like a red-hot coal imbedded in the center of Russ's soul.

Getting drunk hadn't alleviated his grief, and waking to the ringing of the telephone at such an ungodly hour had not started off his day well. Being awake meant facing his actions from the perspective of sobriety, and when he took a good look at his behavior the night before, he could think of no convincing excuse. He'd been taught better.

Another memory flashed through his pounding head. Himself, on the dance floor, loud and laughing. Telling jokes and being generally obnoxious. Jeez, had he really done the macarena with that hot little Spanish number?

That guilt and a belated embarrassment combined with his physical aches and pains to raise his level of crankiness. He wondered again what was so important it called for Logan to make an eight o'clock appointment on Saturday. The happiness he'd heard in his brother's voice had only added to Russ's misery. He couldn't imagine Logan stooping to such unruly behavior—it might muss his fifty-dollar haircut.

As soon as he thought it, Russ dismissed the thought as unfair. In his own way, Logan was as tough as Russ, something he'd learned recently when they'd gone a round over Logan's behavior toward Bliss.

Logan wasn't a sissy, he was just...*polished*. Always an early riser, he'd probably licked the pro at the country club in a couple of sets of tennis, showered, read the paper and made the company several thousand dollars. And it was barely eight o'clock.

Russ jabbed the elevator button. Whatever Logan wanted, it wouldn't be long before Russ's curiosity was satisfied. The elevator trundled to a stop. He eyed the small cubicle warily.

Used to the wide open spaces of the oilfields, he wasn't fond of confinement in any form. When they were kids, Logan had teased him about being claustrophobic, but after receiving a couple of bloody noses for the taunts, he'd stopped. Elevators were a special bugaboo—especially elevators that had been installed just after the turn of the century.

Russ lifted the fancy grillwork gate, stepped inside, slammed it shut and grimly pressed the button for the top floor, where Logan's offices were situated. Then he closed his eyes and leaned against the back wall while the beast lumbered upward, wheezing, groaning and giving an occasional lurch.

A familiar *ping* told him he'd made this trip without mishap. Russ opened his eyes. Though Logan assured him the cables were kept in tip-top shape, Russ always fought the urge to drop to his knees and kiss the carpet when he reached his destination.

Instead, he straightened his shoulders, got out of the cubicle and made his way past the empty receptionist's desk toward his brother's private domain.

The Gaspard Building might be old, but the architect who had designed the structure had kept an eye cocked to the future, and no expense had been spared in its construction. The interior had been redecorated at necessary intervals, and no one would guess from the sleek interior that the building was a hundred years old. Granite and marble never went out of style.

With his hand raised to knock, Russ frowned. The sound of conversation told him there was someone in the room besides his brother. He shrugged and rapped on the heavy oak door.

He was already turning the knob when Logan called for him to enter. To Russ's surprise, there were three men in the room. His brother, who for once had forsaken his sleek businessman's image in favor of casual attire, sat behind a massive mahogany desk.

The dark-haired, mustached man in denim and cowboy boots sprawled on the burgundy leather sofa was Jake Lattimer, a longtime friend.

Russ's gaze moved to the man at the window, who also wore traditional Western garb. The man turned slowly, almost hesitantly. Russ felt his jaw go slack with shock. The guy was a dead ringer for Jake. Or was *he* Jake? Giving serious consideration to the idea that maybe he was still drunk, Russ whipped off his sunglasses and allowed his stunned gaze to move from one man to the other.

The man on the sofa rose, his hand extended in greeting. "Hello, Russ. How are you? It's been a long time."

Russ took the proffered hand automatically. This, then, was Jake. One question solved.

"Fine, Jake. How 'bout you?"

"Never better," Jake said with a smile.

Russ's gaze shifted from his friend to the man across the room. Who the hell was *that?* He must have voiced the question aloud, because Jake answered.

"Zach Rawlings, my twin brother."

Rawlings, who didn't look any more comfortable than Russ felt, gave a brief nod. "You don't have a twin brother," Russ said.

Jake dropped onto the sofa. One corner of his mustache climbed upward in a slow, mocking smile. "Yeah, that's what I thought, too, until some DNA tests proved otherwise."

Russ's throbbing head gave a slow spin. Jake and this Zach person twins? He looked at Logan. "What does this have to do with me?"

Logan glanced at Jake with a look that seemed to

say the explanation was all his. Jake's eyes held an apology as he leaned forward and rested his elbows on his knees.

"I hate to break it to you like this, old buddy, but it's starting to look like Jack Campbell wasn't your father, after all. He's mine." He waved a hand toward his twin. "Ours."

Russ didn't say anything for several seconds. Couldn't. The idea was too preposterous to even consider. The trio looked at him, waiting for a response. He gave them one.

"Are you out of your ever-lovin' mind?" he yelled. The noise sent shock waves through his head.

"'Fraid not," Jake said.

Russ looked to Logan for an answer.

"You don't look so good," Logan said. "Why don't you sit down?"

"No, thanks," Russ snapped.

"Suit yourself." Turning to Zach, Logan said, "Maybe you ought to explain, since you're the one who has most of the pieces."

Zach Rawlings crossed the room and sat next to Jake. Any lingering doubt that the two were brothers—twin brothers—vanished. Russ thought of Logan's offer to sit and eased his hip onto the corner of the gleaming desk.

Zach Rawlings, who Russ learned was a Texas Ranger, began with the tale of how he'd been involved in a sting operation when Georgia, the woman who was now his wife, had mistaken him for Jake.

Listening to the soap opera-ish tale, Russ vaguely remembered hearing something about Jake and Georgia breaking up, but it hadn't made much of an impact on him at the time. Now that he thought about it, he might have even heard about Jake finding a long-lost twin, but he'd been too upset over Bliss's decision to leave Campbell Drilling, Jack's death and Logan's and Bliss's plane crash—not to mention the two of them falling for each other—to be more than mildly intrigued by the news.

"It's an interesting tale," Russ said when he'd heard all the facts, "but I still don't see how you got the harebrained idea that Jack Campbell isn't my dad."

Zach Rawlings shifted uncomfortably. It was clear to Russ that he was choosing his words with care.

"I have a...friend, a reporter in Dallas," he said, "who's really good at digging into this sort of thing. She's been trying to get to the bottom of this for weeks, and she came across some information a few days ago that made most of the bits and pieces come together."

"And what was that?"

"The nurse on duty the night we were all born told her that a young girl named Abby Pickett gave away one of her twin sons because he had a heart condition—"

Despite his skepticism, Russ's heart gave a lurch.

"—and she knew she couldn't handle the medical bills. She agreed to let Ben Lattimer adopt that child so he could get proper medical care. As we all know, Ben adopted Jake, but he's never had a day's problem with his heart."

"And you do—or did," Logan said, cutting to the chase.

Russ stood and faced the three men, his face set with anger. "So based on that, this hotshot reporter decided that we were—what? Switched or something?''

"It was a small country hospital," Logan said, ever ready to see the logic of the situation. "They were understaffed, there was a storm, and the doctor never made it. The nurse delivered all of us, and we were all born within an hour or so of each other—the two of us just before midnight, Jake and Zach just after. It would have been easy to get confused.''

"If you watch any television at all, you know that what Logan's saying isn't that farfetched," Jake added.

Fury swept through Russ. He was still trying to deal with Jack's death. He didn't want to hear that the man who'd carried him on his shoulders, the man who'd blistered his butt when he did something wrong, the man who'd taught him everything he knew about bringing in an oil well wasn't his father.

"You're all crazy," he said, heading for the door. "Jack Campbell was my father."

"Russ, listen..." Logan began.

Gripping the doorknob, Russ turned, his face set in familiar, stubborn lines, a forefinger aimed at his brother. "No, *you* listen. There's no way two people could be as close as Jack and I were without the same blood flowing in our veins. I don't know what's going on, but I'm damn sure going to find out."

Logan dropped his head into his hands in defeat. Zach and Jake stared at Russ, twin expressions of misery on their faces. Finally Russ shoved his sunglasses onto his nose, turned the knob and exited the room, slamming the door behind him.

"I'd say he didn't take it too well," Jake observed as the vibrations died.

"He's a hardhead," Logan said.

"He needs time," Zach told them. "Remember how we felt a few weeks ago, Jake?"

Jake nodded. "I'll never forget it."

"It's especially tough for him since we just lost Jack," Logan said.

"Don't forget that Zach and I lost him, too," Jake said.

Logan thrust a hand through his hair and gave a short laugh. "Yeah, I guess you did. I keep waiting for someone to jump out and say, 'Surprise! You're on *Candid Camera.*'"

"I don't think that's gonna happen, pal," Zach said, a cold bleakness in his eyes.

Logan didn't answer, but deep in his heart, he didn't, either.

Russ was so furious he hardly noticed the elevator ride to the lobby or the city noises that greeted him outside the building. He reached into his pocket for the keys to the pickup that, at this time on a Saturday morning, claimed a premier parking spot directly in front of the building.

The interior was already starting to warm up. He put the key into the ignition but hesitated turning it. He wasn't sure where he wanted to go. The hunger plaguing him earlier was gone, and his mind roiled with the nonsense he'd just heard.

He sank against the seat back and clasped the nape of his neck to massage the tightening muscles. Of all the stupid, idiotic ideas! He didn't doubt there was a mix-up somewhere, but it was beyond him how anyone, including Logan—*especially* Logan—could believe Jack and Valerie Campbell were not their real parents.

Russ straightened. His mother! He'd go and talk to her, tell her what he'd just heard. She'd know if she brought her own babies home or not. She'd ease his mind and set everyone straight.

By habit, Russ parked near the four-car garage at the rear of the Gaspard mansion and crossed the few short steps to the kitchen entrance. A peek through the back door revealed Sophie, his mother's cook for the past twenty years, bustling around the bright, airy kitchen. He watched as she poured coffee from a modern glass carafe into a flower-sprinkled Spode coffeepot and set it on a wicker breakfast tray next to a silver-covered dish, a small Wedgwood vase filled with fresh flowers and the current edition of the *Times-Picayune*. His mother must be having breakfast in bed.

He knocked twice and opened the door before Sophie could respond with more than a smile.

"What are you doing out so bright and early?" she asked, giving him a brief hug. "We didn't expect you until this afternoon."

"I had a meeting with Logan."

"On a Saturday?" Sophie tsked. "I thought he'd slowed down since he and Miss Bliss decided to tie the knot."

Russ's foul mood lifted a bit at the mention of his foster sister. "Is Baby Sister here?"

Sophie shook her head. "She flew up to New York to look for a wedding dress."

A wicked smile curved Russ's lips at the thought of his rough-and-tumble sister with her strong opinions and her barbed tongue descending on the unsuspecting city. "Fifth Avenue will never be the same."

"You can say that again," Sophie said, turning to pick up the breakfast tray.

"I'll take that," Russ said, reaching for the tray. His concerned gaze met her faded blue eyes. "Is she okay, Sophie?"

"Your mama?"

Russ nodded. Valerie was no spoiled debutante who demanded breakfast in bed.

"She's a little under the weather with one of her headaches."

Though his mother was a rock whenever something went wrong in her world, managing to rise to every difficult occasion, sometimes life managed to bring her down with a stress-related headache that sent her to bed. "Is something wrong?"

Sophie shrugged. "I couldn't say. Logan came to visit her late yesterday, and she took to her bed not long afterward."

An unaccountable feeling of foreboding settled in the pit of Russ's stomach. Had Logan already discussed Zach Rawlings's theory with their mom?

Sophie pursed her lips. "I haven't seen her so upset since she and your daddy split up. She wasn't even this distraught when he died."

"I think those few days he seemed to be getting better gave her time to prepare herself for his passing," Russ said.

"Maybe so." Sophie patted his shoulder as he reached into the cabinet for a utilitarian LSU mug that said Geaux Tigers. "Maybe you can cheer her up."

Russ dredged up a smile. "I'll try."

He picked up the tray and took the service stairs

two at a time, stopping outside his mother's room and knocking on the door.

"Come in."

He expected to find her in bed, but she stood at the window, clad in tailored satin pajamas and a matching robe of burgundy and deep rose, staring at the formal gardens at the back of the house.

"Are you all right?"

She whirled at the sound of his voice, her hand going to her throat in a familiar gesture of surprise. "Russell! What are you doing here?"

"I need to talk to you."

She tried to smile. Failed. "I need to talk to you, too, *chèr*," she said, her voice little more than a whisper.

. Fighting a sudden, foreign sense of panic, he set the tray on the bed. When he turned, his mother stood no more than a foot from him. He hadn't heard her bare feet cross the carpet.

They stared at each other while the gilded antique clock on her bedside table ticked away the seconds. The vulnerability he saw in her dark eyes reflected the rawness of his emotions. Without a word, Russ pulled her close and rested his cheek against the top of her head. He felt her arms circle his waist and breathed in the familiar scent of her perfume. She trembled in his arms. For the first time in his life, he was struck by her fragility.

Without warning, a memory of when he was nine years old surfaced. His mom and dad were getting a divorce. Knowing their lives were about to change, but not truly understanding how much, he and Logan had huddled in bed night after night, listening to long hours of arguing and doing their best to hide their tears and fears.

In the end, his parents decided to split the family as well as their property, one child for each parent. Russ was to go with Jack. Logan would stay with Valerie. Russ would never forget the stoic expression on his brother's face when Jack made the announcement, or the pain in Logan's eyes and the telltale tremble of his lower lip when he'd begged Jack to take him, too.

Russ had done his own share of tearful pleading with his dad. If Logan couldn't go, couldn't he *please* stay with his mother and brother? Their feelings hadn't seemed to matter. Russ remembered Jack telling him this way was the best for everyone, remembered Valerie holding him as she was holding him now—tightly, as if she'd never let him go. Couldn't let him go. But in the end, she had…as she did now.

The tightness in his chest forced him to push away the memories. He stepped back and pressed a kiss to her forehead.

"You've talked to Logan?" she asked.

"Yeah. What the hell's going on, Mom?"

Valerie brushed at the tears glistening on her lashes and laced her fingers together. "I'm not sure I know," she confessed. "All I know is what Logan told me. They were looking into Zach and Jake's…separation…"

Her voice broke, and she paused, compressing her lips for a moment before she could continue. "Evidently, I told the reporter some things that made her suspect there was a mix-up that night."

Suddenly, Russ realized that if the ridiculous scenario proved true, Valerie had been denied raising her own children. The agony in her eyes kept him silent. She didn't need him flying off the handle.

"Why don't I pour us some coffee while you give me the *Reader's Digest* version of what this reporter person thinks happened?"

Valerie crossed the ivory carpet and sat on a pillow-strewn sofa covered in ivory damask. Russ joined her, balancing his mug on his denim-clad thigh.

"Your dad and I were on our way from Louisiana to Oklahoma the night you were born. I was due in a couple of weeks, but there was no way he was leaving me behind. I started having contractions just outside Shreveport, near the Texas line. By the time Jack saw the hospital in Brownsboro, I was carrying on so he thought he'd better stop."

"Carrying on?" Russ asked with a lifted eyebrow. "You?"

"As I recall, I wasn't very good at that part," Valerie said, offering him a bittersweet smile. "I remember that it was storming like crazy and there was no doctor at the hospital. The phone lines were down, and there was just this Raquel Welch look-alike nurse who examined me and gave me something for the pain."

"Without doctor's orders?"

"Good point. But it was a dinky hospital, and I was hurting so badly, I was begging for relief. Jack said I was acting like a wild woman." Valerie laughed. "I remember being afraid the sexy nurse would make a move on him while I was in labor."

As he listened, Russ felt his confidence that his mom could set things straight begin to waver. "So you were out of it during the actual birth?"

She nodded. "I have a vague memory of someone

telling me I had a boy, and then, a little later, saying there were two boys. I remember being surprised. I was so *huge*, but I wasn't expecting twins. It was before ultrasound, and my doctor never heard but one heartbeat.''

''What else do you remember?''

''Nothing, really, except what Jack told me later. Ben and Retha Lattimer were in there, waiting to hear about the baby they were adopting. The nurse told them they'd be taking home a boy, too.''

''They didn't know he was a twin?''

''Obviously not. Not until a few weeks ago.''

''And you didn't—I don't know—feel that something was wrong when you held me and Logan?''

''You have to remember none of us had any idea there was another set of twins born that night. Why would we even imagine something like that happening?''

She shook her head, smiling fondly at a distant memory. ''You and Logan were beautiful and healthy and had all your fingers and toes—you were also bald. When your hair came in auburn and Logan's was sandy blond, we thought it would change as you got older. When it didn't, we chalked it up to recessive genes.''

Russ nodded, starting to see that this terrible thing might have happened, after all.

''The nurse who delivered me told you I had a heart problem?''

''No. Jack was anxious to be on his way, and foolishly, we left the hospital the next day. It was a few days later, after we got settled in Oklahoma, that I had you both checked over and the doctor there discovered a small hole in your heart.

"It had closed up by the time your dad and I divorced, but by then I was so accustomed to treating you like an invalid it was hard to break the habit." Valerie smiled apologetically. "That's why Jack insisted on taking you when we split up. He knew Logan was tough, but he said that if he didn't get you away from me and my coddling, you'd wind up a sissy, and that's one thing Jack Campbell just couldn't take."

"I thought you sent me with Dad because you were tired of me being sick all the time."

Valerie's shock couldn't have been clearer. "Oh, Russell, no! I didn't sleep for weeks after you left. It broke my heart when Jack took you, even though I knew he was right and I was doing exactly what he said I was."

Knowing Jack as well as he had, her claim made sense. Russ recalled the first year or so after he'd left Louisiana, and how, when life didn't go just right or he started missing Valerie, he'd cry that his chest hurt. Jack's answer had always been that there wasn't a damn thing wrong, so he'd better stop whining and do as he was told.

His dad's attitude had hurt, but Russ had sucked it up and obeyed. After a while, knowing he'd get no sympathy, Russ had stopped complaining.

"I remember him telling me I was okay, but I never really believed him—not after the way you babied me for so long. He never once sat me down and explained that I'd outgrown the condition." Russ smiled, a quick, humorless lift of his lips. "Until a few years ago, I lived my life expecting to drop dead any minute."

"That's so like Jack. So you decided that if you

were going to die young, you'd just live fast and love hard, huh?'' Valerie said, her smile matching his.

Russ nodded. "About the same time I realized I'd get no sympathy from Dad, I decided I'd make his life the hell he'd made mine. I thought that if I was bad enough, he'd send me back to you."

Tears filled Valerie's eyes. She reached out, took Russ's hand in hers. Neither spoke for a moment. Finally, he said, "I went through a spell when I thought I hated you for choosing Logan. And I resented him for having you. Did you know that?"

"I knew." The softly uttered acknowledgment was accompanied by a sorrowful smile. "It started when you were twelve or thirteen. About the time Logan started feeling the same way about you and Jack."

She shook her head. "Lord, he worshiped Jack. *He* thought Jack loved *you* more. I don't think I ever made him understand that how we felt about you boys had nothing to do with our decision to separate you."

Valerie looked as if she were about to cry again. "In retrospect, we shouldn't have done that. Logan resents that he's been confined to offices and company business all these years, when he'd far rather have been out on a rig." She brushed at her eyes. "Sometimes I think I should have let Jack take you both, but I just couldn't bear not having one of you with me."

Even though he and Logan had come a long way in resolving their differences since Jack's death, Russ felt the lingering remnants of an old insecurity lift from his shoulders. "Well, we've both grown up, and we understand. There's been no permanent harm done to either of us."

"Who's to say?" Valerie said with a rueful shake

of her head. "It's a frightening reality that parents have their children for approximately eighteen years and that everything they do to and for them during that short time affects them for the rest of their lives, even if they live to be a hundred."

"Don't be so hard on yourself, Mom," he said, giving her fingers a squeeze. "I'm not *too* warped."

As he'd hoped, Valerie laughed. "By the grace of God. I pray that you and Logan do better with your families."

Seeing that she was still struggling with her tears, Russ didn't say anything for a moment. "You believe it, then? That we were switched?" he asked at last.

Valerie's teeth clamped down hard on her bottom lip. She nodded. Controlling her emotions with an effort, she said, "Jake and Zach look so much like Jack. I can't believe I didn't see it before."

Russ's heart sank. He felt nine years old again, watching out the back window of his dad's pickup truck while his mother grew smaller and smaller in the distance.

Valerie saw the hopelessness in his eyes. "Russell," she said gently. "You have to know that whatever relationship develops between me and Jake and Zach, nothing could make me love you and Logan any less."

"I know that," he told her, and deep in his heart, he did. Still, he realized there were some shocks and major adjustments ahead.

"It's really ironic," she said thoughtfully. "If I hadn't mentioned to Laura that you and Logan were twins, she might never have put the pieces together."

Laura? Everything stopped—pain, time, Russ's heart. "Did you say Laura?"

"Yes. Laura Ramirez. The reporter. I talked with her a week or so ago. Why? Do you know her?"

He gave a slow nod. "We met when she covered the Odessa blowout six years ago."

Laura had been sent from San Antonio to cover the raging well fire in Odessa. She was there when one of the firefighters succumbed to the blistering heat and passed out. She was there when Russ pulled the man to safety. She'd seen him don the man's fire-fighting gear and take his place. She'd watched while, beneath the streams of water, he'd edged the dozer nearer, situating the crane with the nitro so they could blow out the fire and cap the well.

He surged to his feet. "Look, Mom, I've got to go."

"Will you be all right?"

All right? He wasn't sure he'd ever be all right again. And hearing that Laura was the person responsible for bearing the bad news had shaken his world pretty badly. He needed to go somewhere to think about what he'd heard and to try to make some sense of it.

"I'm fine," he lied. "How about you?"

"It will take some getting used to. Maybe," she suggested, "we should all try to get together and...I don't know...talk this out."

Talk? Why was it that women always wanted to talk about problems, and men just wanted to punch someone? "Sure. Soon," he said. He kissed her good-bye and left before she could tell him any more shocking news.

This was all happening too fast. Everyone was buying into the baby-switching thing way too easily to suit him. He tried to ignore the fact that Laura's theory about a woman giving up one baby because of a heart condition, which he just happened to have, was pretty strong support for her case.

A new thought stole his breath. If Jake and Zach were really Jack and Valerie's sons, he and Logan had no idea who *their* birth parents were! He felt a shift in his soul as the crack in the foundation of his world widened.

He'd always been a Campbell. Damn it, he *was* a Campbell! Laura Ramirez had no right to dig into things that didn't concern her, no business going around destroying other people's lives.

Valerie had asked if he knew Laura. He knew her, all right…in every sense of the word. His actions at Odessa—she said he was either a hero or a fool, depending on how you looked at it—had impressed her. Everything about her had impressed him.

They didn't know each other long, but during the weeks following the fire, he'd learned to know her well.

He knew that she was a top-notch reporter who gave every assignment her all, and more. There was no detail too small not to investigate, no piece of information too meaningless not to check out. He knew she was loyal, dedicated, driven to succeed.

He knew she liked to laugh, and that her compact, curvaceous body delivered on its sexy promise. He knew she went crazy when he kissed a certain spot behind her knees and that she liked to cuddle in the aftermath of lovemaking.

They were together for six weeks before the heat of their passion burned itself out. No, that wasn't exactly true. Russ suspected that would never happen.

What really came between them was the reality of life.

After meeting her, Russ had all but abandoned Campbell Drilling, spending more time on the road to rendezvous with Laura than he did at the well site. Finally, Jack had told him to make a choice, the woman or his job.

Russ had known Laura was crazy about him. She'd even hinted about marriage a time or two. But he'd always been a love-'em-and-leave-'em kind of guy, and even though the thought of being separated from her for any length of time was almost more than he could bear, the depth of his feelings for her had him running scared. It had happened too fast. It was too perfect, too good to be true. Past relationships had burned out in a few months. He had no reason to think this one would be any different.

His solution was to suggest that she follow him from town to town and rig to rig and wait for him in the local motel. But Laura let him know real fast that she was no oil-well groupie. She had her own plans for the future, and while they included marriage at some point, she didn't intend to be any man's after-hours plaything.

He hadn't slept for weeks after they split up. His distraction at the site made working with him dangerous. He was ordered to take an extended vacation until he could get his head on straight. He was gone—to Australia, Africa and South America—for more than six months. It was that long before he met a woman who interested him enough ask out, more than a year before he forged any kind of ongoing relationship. But even now, after six years, he could honestly say that not one woman made him feel the things Laura Ramirez did.

She was still making him feel, he realized, but it was pain this time, not passion. He'd like to tell her exactly what she could do with her adoption article and the stupid supposition that someone had switched him and Logan with Zach and Jake.

Maybe he would.

The audacity of the thought stole his breath. His heart began to beat faster. Maybe he'd just do that. Look her up and tell her what he thought about her and her damned investigative reporting.

But even as he thought it, he knew that, deep in his heart, he wanted more than to give her a piece of his mind. He wanted to lose himself in the liquid warmth of her brown eyes...just one more time.

Chapter Three

"You're sure he's okay?"

"Positive."

"Okay. Thanks again, sis. Bye."

Laura shut the door behind her sister, relieved that J.R.—Rufio—had had a good day. The thought of her baby having a heart condition was terrifying, but he'd been under the weather since spring, suffering from weariness and lethargy and sporadic bouts of nausea, and it was a relief to finally know what the problem was.

Though the pediatrician had run scores of tests the past few weeks and considered everything from a strong susceptibility to every virus to come along to neurological problems, it wasn't until Rufio had a spell in the hospital that a pediatric heart specialist had put his finger on the problem, a condition called tachycardia, symptomized by runaway heart rate.

Laura had been terrified to hear the news, but when the doctor explained that the condition could be controlled with medication and was often outgrown, her fears leveled off.

She was still protective, though, and didn't want him staying with the regular sitter just yet. Thankfully, Inez, whose three kids were in school, had offered to keep J.R. at home indefinitely.

The sounds of squealing tires and crashes wafted through the house. Laura smiled and started toward her son's room. After the day she'd had, it was nice to come home and know he was curled up in his room killing off space invaders or wrecking cars on his Nintendo.

"Hola, niño," she said, poking her head through the open doorway.

"Hi, Mom!" Rufio said, bestowing a dimpled smile so much like his father's that it stole her breath. Sometimes his resemblance to Russ was frightening, and she suspected the similarities would only grow more marked the older the boy got.

"How do you feel?"

Rufio deigned to look up from the screen long enough to scowl at her. "Fine."

"If you feel well enough to be grouchy, I suppose that's a good sign," Laura said with a smile. "What do you want for dinner?"

"Peanut butter and jelly."

Peanut butter and red plum jam was Rufio's new favorite food. Sometimes she thought he'd turn into a peanut butter and jelly sandwich. "No way, José," she said. "Tia Inez said you had that for lunch. How about some chicken on the grill?"

Rufio shrugged.

"I take it that's a yes." When he didn't answer, she said, "I'm going to change clothes and start dinner. I'll be in the kitchen if you need me."

He nodded and, with a sigh, she turned and went across the hall to her bedroom where she changed into a pair of cutoffs and a sleeveless blouse of vivid teal. She took the pins from her hair and clipped the dark, curling mass on top of her head. Barefoot, she padded through the small tract house to the kitchen, pausing to lower the thermostat on the way.

The day had been hot and long, one of those rare and beautiful Indian summer days with skies so bright and clear it made your eyes hurt. Of course, she'd never have known that if she'd spent the day in the city instead of interviewing one of Abby Pickett's old boyfriends.

When Laura had phoned Chip Brownlee the day before, she'd been vague about her reason for setting up the interview, saying she wanted to talk to him about some of his former classmates for an article she was writing. His interest piqued and, she suspected, his ego involved, Chip had agreed to give her an hour of his time—if Laura would drive to his ranch in Palestine. Though it was Saturday, she'd agreed.

Clayton "Chip" Brownlee looked like a former football hero, which, her research had proven, he was—at least on the college level. He'd been scouted by the pros, and if not for a severe knee injury his senior year at SMU, he might have been a prime draft pick.

Unfortunately for her, Chip—now over fifty but still a handsome man—was eaten up with what Laura had come to think of as "jock mentality." After they'd gone through the requisite let's-see-if-I-can-score-with-you routine and Laura had kept him firmly in his place, Chip, his colossal ego a bit bruised, had resorted to cool disdain.

"You mentioned wanting to talk about some of my classmates. What's the article about, anyway?" he asked, sipping a glass of diet cola.

"I'm calling it 'Adoption—Then and Now,'" she told him. "It's about the changes that have taken place in adoption policies over the past fifty years."

Chip spun the glass in the condensation that had collected on the glass-topped table. "I'm afraid you've wasted your time, Ms. Ramirez. I can't possibly give you any insight on that topic."

"I'm specifically interested in Abby Pickett," Laura said. "Do you remember her?"

"Sure I do, but what does she have to do with the article?"

"You must have known she got pregnant, went away and came back several months later with a baby."

Chip nodded. "Yeah."

"Inadvertently, I found out she gave birth to twins."

"No kidding!" By all appearances, Chip's surprise was genuine. "But she just brought one baby home," he said thoughtfully. Then, as if a light bulb had gone off inside his head, he nodded. "Ah. Here's where the adoption part comes in, right?"

"Right."

"Why *did* she give up one baby and not the other?"

"That's a good question," Laura said. "From what I've learned, she planned to give up her baby, but when the time came, she couldn't go through with it.

She must have talked her parents into letting her keep them, but when she found out one had a heart problem, I figure she knew her family couldn't afford the medical bills, so she agreed to adopt the sick one out."

"Makes sense," Brownlee said, nodding. "The Picketts didn't have a lot of money. But I still don't see what this has to do with me."

"It should be obvious. I'm curious to know if you're the father of Abby Pickett's babies."

Brownlee gaped at her as if she'd just grown another head. "You've got to be kidding."

"I assure you, Mr. Brownlee, that the two men looking for their birth father don't find it at all humorous, and you were dating Abby back then."

"Yeah, me and a couple of other guys dated her that year. Abby and I even went steady for a few months." He laughed. "But me getting Abby pregnant is a joke. I never even got in her pants, Ms. Ramirez, and that's the truth. Her dad did a good job of teaching her to practice what he preached. In fact, I broke up with her so I could move on to an easier mark."

"So it wasn't you?"

He shook his head. "I was shocked to find out she was pregnant. We all were. And we all wondered who she'd finally given in to. I knew a few of my friends thought it was me." Chip had the grace to look shamefaced. "I confess I didn't tell them any differently. It was a macho thing. But it wasn't me, I swear."

For some reason she couldn't put her finger on, Laura believed him. Disappointment flooded her. Would she ever find out who had fathered Logan and

Russ? "Can you give me the names of the other guys she dated?"

"Sure, but I don't think it will help. One of them is a priest now, and he was pretty religious even back then. The other died a few years ago in a car wreck."

Laura rubbed her throbbing temples. "Did she ever mention anyone else? Maybe a guy from another town, another school?"

"No. After we broke up she got this baby-sitting job that paid pretty good, and that took up a lot of her weekends, so she only dated Bob and Gene occasionally."

"Okay. Can you give me the names of her closest friends? Maybe she shared the guy's name with one of her girlfriends."

"Sure." Chip took a small notepad from his shirt pocket and scribbled a couple of names. "The last high school reunion I went to, they both still lived in the area."

Laura stuck the piece of paper in her purse, stood and extended her hand. "Thanks for your time, Mr. Brownlee."

"My pleasure," he'd said with another winning smile. "Sorry I couldn't be more help."

Brownlee might have been sorry, but not as sorry as she'd been, Laura thought as she put the chicken for her and Rufio's dinner on the gas grill.

The day before, she'd held a brief phone conversation with an old nurse who'd worked with Lillian at the Brownsboro hospital, but she hadn't gleaned any information from her except that Lillian could be difficult to work under, that she was a sharp dresser and her mother had been put into an exclusive nursing home when she'd developed Alzheimer's.

Disappointed, Laura carried the empty platter inside and washed her hands. She'd pinned her hopes on Brownlee. Now she'd hit another dead end. Once she called the women whose names Chip had given her, she'd be out of leads.

She was drying her hands when the doorbell rang. She growled in frustration. Sometimes she was positive that every salesman and telemarketer in the world knew what time she got home from work. There was no sense telling Rufio to get it. From the sounds coming from the bedroom, he was involved in a sprightly game of Tetras.

With a sigh, she went to the front door and stood on tiptoe to check the peephole. A shoulder, which was all she could see, belonged to a man. A new truck was at the curb. The visitor might be a serial killer looking for his next mark, but if so, he was one with money. More than likely, her impromptu caller was some society dude doing his bit for the Heart Association.

She swung the door open, a false smile of greeting on her face.

The man turned. His amber eyes darkened to the hue of aged honey.

Her smile slipped.

Russ. The ancient instinct to protect herself and her young rushed through her. She didn't think, she reacted, swinging the door shut with all the force she could muster.

The heavy oak smacked into the palm of a strong, outstretched hand and went crashing against the wall so hard the pictures rattled. Laura gasped and took a step back as he surged into the room, stopping less than a yard from her.

She drew in a shuddering breath. He looked wonderful—from the top of his tousled auburn head down to his snug-fitting jeans and the toes of his battered Nike sneakers.

He looked terrible. Like a prizefighter. Or a thug. He had a black eye, a bruise on his jaw and a cut and swollen bottom lip.

He was everything she remembered and more. Bigger. Bolder. Badder. And so darn sexy she could have seduced him on the spot...if J.R. hadn't been in the other room.

J.R. Someone had let it slip about J.R. Laura fought a wave of panic. She had to get Russ out of the house before he saw J.R.—before J.R. saw him. She wasn't ready for this. She hadn't had time to prepare herself. She hadn't perfected her stiff little confession, hadn't—

"How dare you suggest such a stupid idea and screw up so many lives!" Russ said in an embittered tone.

Laura blinked. Whatever she'd expected him to say, this wasn't it.

"All to make a name for yourself, right, Laura? You always did put your damned career ahead of your personal feelings. Anything to get the scoop."

Knee-weakening relief overcame her panic. He wasn't there to demand the details about J.R.'s existence. He was there because of what she'd uncovered about him and Logan being switched with Jake and Zach.

"What's the matter?" he taunted. "At a loss for words? Eaten up with guilt?" He reached out and took her by the shoulders, spinning her around and pinning her against the wall. She sucked in a startled breath. Even in anger, his touch ignited fires she thought she'd buried beneath years of mind-numbing work.

She looked at him, her breasts heaving as she dragged huge gulps of air into her lungs. She closed her eyes against the fury reflected in his. Her tongue skimmed over her dry lips.

He growled a curse and took her chin in a hard grip.

"Look at me...ouch!"

His grip loosened, and his head whipped sideways so he could see over his shoulder. Laura gasped. Rufio's thin arms were clamped to Russ's denim-clad leg, his teeth sunk into the side of Russ's thigh with all the ferocity of a pit bull. Russ tried to shake him off, but J.R. wrapped his legs more tightly around Russ's calf. With a curse, Russ reached down and grabbed Rufio by the shoulders. He growled low in his throat.

"Don't you dare touch him—" Laura cried, finding her voice and moving out of Russ's reach. She wasn't as afraid he'd hurt J.R. as she was fearful that the excitement would cause the child to have another attack.

"Then get the little brat off me."

"Rufio!" Laura said sharply. "Let go. I'm all right."

Rufio, his teeth still buried in denim, cut his gaze to her.

"It's all right, *niño*." She squatted and held out her arms. "Come."

Reluctantly, J.R. released his death grip on the in-

truder and ran into Laura's waiting arms. Russ
reached down and rubbed his mutilated flesh, his gaze
fixed on her and the boy. "Who the hell is that?"

Safe in her embrace, Rufio turned and faced his
adversary. Before Laura could answer, Russ uttered a
soft, "Dear God!"

There was no use fabricating a lie. Nor did she have
to search for the right words to tell him J.R. was his
son. The look on his face said that he'd already figured it out.

Transfixed, Russ stared at the child in Laura's
arms. If the kid wasn't his, he'd give up his share of
Campbell Drilling.

"My name is James Russell Ramirez!" the boy
yelled, defiance in his amber-hued eyes.

If there were any lingering doubts in Russ's mind,
the announcement dispelled them. This was his son,
and Laura had kept his existence a secret for six years.

"Damn you," he muttered to her in a low, fierce
voice.

Sensing a threat to his mother, Rufio gave another
of those low, feral growls. Russ took a step back.

Without speaking, Laura stood, shifting the boy to
her left hip. His legs dangled down hers. He was tall
for his age, which Russ calculated would be five.

"Why didn't you tell me?"

"Not now, Russ." She spoke from between
clenched teeth, cutting her gaze toward the child in
warning.

Russ's gaze hardened. "Now."

Dark eyes blazing, she rattled off a string of Spanish. Russ knew just enough to know she was cursing
him and his lineage.

"Wait here," she snapped, turning on the ball of a bare foot. The boy, his arms wound tightly around her neck, glared at Russ over her shoulder and stuck out his tongue.

Varied and violent emotions tumbled through Russ—shock that he and Laura had created a child, fury at her for depriving him of that knowledge for so many years, maybe even a bit of pride. He couldn't help admiring how the kid stood up to him, even though it was clear he could use a little more discipline.

While Laura argued with the child in the bedroom, Russ looked around the small living room, willing his anger to abate and hoping to slake some of his curiosity about what she'd done with herself since they parted.

Though no specific decorating style had emerged, the room, with its traditional cream and forest green striped sofa, Monet prints and an abundance of green plants, was tastefully furnished.

Russ knew the neighborhood was old but respectable. Laura might not have won the Pulitzer, but she had done okay.

Maybe it isn't her. Maybe it's her husband. The thought of her being married brought back his scowl. He couldn't remember if she'd worn a ring on her left hand or not.

"I'm sorry I was so long," she said, her voice preceding her into the room. "Rufio can be awfully headstrong sometimes."

"Rufio? I thought he was named after me." Even Russ heard the censure in his voice.

Laura's face flamed. He saw the imperceptible lift of her chin. She raised her hand and pushed her hair from her face in a familiar gesture. Her left hand. No ring. The knowledge that there was no husband lightened Russ's heart, though he wouldn't have admitted it—even to himself—under threat of death.

"He *is* named after you," Laura said. "Rufio is a nickname...because of his hair. Most people call him J.R." A hint of a smile flitted across her lips. "For obvious reasons."

Even in his anger Russ felt another jolt of male pride. The kid must be a real pistol! "That bad, huh?"

The unexpected lightness of his tone caught her off guard. The bit of softness in her eyes vanished, and she straightened visibly. Her voice could have frosted the windows. "Let's just say he does an excellent job of living up to it."

They stood for a moment, each struggling for a civilized way to proceed. "Do you mind if I sit down?" Russ finally asked.

"I'd rather you didn't."

He felt the rekindling of his anger. "Fine." He shifted his weight to one leg, crossed his arms and pinned her with an intense look. "At the risk of being redundant, why didn't you tell me?"

"Why should I have?" Laura said, her dark eyes flashing. "So you could tell me to go get an abortion?"

The idea that she'd think that of him stunned Russ. "I'd never have asked you to do that."

"What would you have done, then?" she challenged.

That, too, took him aback.

"Would you have asked me to marry you, Russ?" Before he could answer, she forged ahead, her eyes burning with defiance and her own brand of pride. "You made it pretty clear that you weren't interested in anything from me but adoration and sex. Somehow I can't see you taking the little Mexican girl from San Antonio to your parents and telling them you wanted to make me a part of the family because I was pregnant."

Russ let his arms fall to his sides. He had no quick comeback to that. He couldn't deny she was right. He hadn't been interested in settling down back then— with anyone. It was only after he'd lost her that he realized how much she'd meant to him.

"It wasn't you or your background," he told her. "I might be a lot of things, but a racist isn't one of them."

"No?" She crossed her arms beneath her breasts, a gesture that drew his eyes to their soft fullness. Soft, full breasts he could plainly see were unbound beneath the cotton of her T-shirt. Breasts he remembered touching. Tasting.

"It was me, not you. I was twenty-nine and full of myself."

"You certainly were. Russ Campbell, rich man's son. Ladies' man. *Hero*." She shook her head. "I still remember how the women crowded around you wherever we went. How you thrived on the attention."

Russ frowned. Women had always flocked to him, for his looks and his money, and as much as it hurt to admit now, he knew he'd taken it for granted. "Was I that bad?"

"Worse."

The blunt honesty of her answer robbed him momentarily of speech before a new thought occurred to him. "If I was so terrible, why did you fall for me?"

It was Laura's turn to be caught off guard. He watched the anger in her dark eyes turn slowly to despair. "I don't know."

The confession hung in the air between them. It was more than an admission that she didn't know why. It was an acknowledgment that she *had* cared. Because Russ found a measure of satisfaction in that concession, he felt he owed her an equally honest answer to her earlier question.

"I'll be the first to admit I was a jerk back then. I thought my interest in you was temporary and sexual. All the others had been."

He dragged a tortured breath into his lungs. Confession might be good for the soul, but it was heck on the nerves. He plowed a hand through his slightly curly hair.

"Knowing I'd fathered a child would have been either a big ego trip or bigger guilt trip. I might have asked you to marry me because I thought it was the right thing to do, or because it was a new boost to my colossal conceit."

She met his gaze unflinchingly. "Either of those reasons would have been the wrong one."

Half a dozen seconds ticked by. "I could have helped you financially."

The unyielding look was back in her eyes. Pride lent stiffness to her voice. "I've done all right. Rufio hasn't had everything he wanted, but he's had more than a lot of kids. Besides, there are more important things than money."

That stung. "I know that," Russ said, keeping a tight hold on his irritation. Damn! He was trying to make amends, and she kept throwing the gesture in his face. "I didn't mean to imply that you hadn't done well by him. Just that helping out financially is the least I could have done."

"You're right. It's the very least you could have done." She put her fists on her hips. "Tell me, Russ. If you'd known about J.R. would you have come to his preschool play or just sent a check from Campbell Drilling to cover the cost of his costume?"

The question lay in his mind like a hot poker.

"Would you go to kindergarten field day to watch him run the sack race? Or attend a parent-teacher conference?"

Russ tried to picture himself sitting next to Laura while they talked to a faceless person about J.R.'s scholastic accomplishments. Tried to imagine himself surrounded by kids and parents while J.R. hopped along in a feed sack. Couldn't.

"Would you come to the Halloween carnival, or would you have just bought some chances to win a Thanksgiving turkey?"

"Damn it, I don't know!" Russ thundered.

"Mama!" Rufio screamed from the bedroom.

Russ's heart sank.

"It's okay, *niño,*" she called, glaring at Russ. "Play your video games."

"Why is he afraid of me?" Russ asked.

"Because he came in here and you had me pinned against the wall. You were yelling. He isn't used to men...or violence."

"Damn it, I'm not violent," Russ said, keeping his voice to a loud whisper.

"No?"

Realizing that his actions exemplified the very behavior he denied, he clasped the back of his neck and turned away. At the door, he turned to face her.

"Would you have ever told me if I hadn't come here today?"

She nodded. "Yes."

Her eyes looked suspiciously bright. "When?"

"Soon," she whispered. She pressed her lips together and turned her back on him.

She was crying! In all the weeks they were together, he'd never seen her cry. An inexplicable dread seeped through him.

Without thinking beyond finding out what had upset her, he crossed to her and took her shoulders in his hands. "What is it?"

Instead of the rebuff he expected, Laura turned toward him. Her eyes swam with unshed tears. "When I talked to your mother the other day, she told me you had a heart problem. Well, I just found out that J.R. does, too."

Russ stood there, trying to absorb the fact that he was already in danger of losing the son he'd just gained. "What kind of heart problem?"

"Tachycardia."

He listened while Laura explained the symptoms J.R. had suffered since late spring and how it had taken scores of tests, a change of doctors and a spell while he was in the hospital to finally diagnose the condition.

"It's manageable with medicine," she said, rubbing her upper arms with her hands, as if she were trying to ward off the same chill that had settled in Russ's bones when she'd first made the announcement. "And he may outgrow it."

"I outgrew mine," Russ said.

Her hopeful gaze flew to his. "You did?"

"It wasn't the same condition, but, yeah, I did. I had a hole in my heart. It closed."

"That's encouraging, isn't it?"

"I'd say so." Russ would have told her the sun set in the east if it would have erased the worry clouding her eyes.

"I want to talk to your mother."

"Who isn't really my mother, according to you," he mocked gently.

Again, she met his censure steadfastly. "No, I don't believe she is."

"Do you have any idea how many people you've hurt by dragging all this up?"

"I know it's painful for everyone, but living a lie is never right."

"You should know."

If he thought the dig would add to her guilt, he was disappointed. She didn't so much as blink an eye. "So where do we go from here?" he asked.

"Logan has asked me to find out who your father is."

"As far as I'm concerned, Jack Campbell was my father."

"You're right, Russ. He was. But have you thought that there may be a man out there somewhere who has no idea you and Logan exist, just the way you had no idea Rufio existed? Have you thought that he might like to know he has twin sons?" She shrugged her shapely shoulders. "Who knows? There might be a chance for some sort of relationship even at this late date."

Russ's jaw tightened. "Count me out. I'm not interested in forging any father-son relationship with some stranger. But Logan's over twenty-one. He can do what he wants.''

"He will." They stared at each other, unwilling to talk more about the past and unable to think of anything else to say. Finally, Russ inclined his head toward the bedroom and asked, "What are you going to tell him about me?"

Resolution gleamed in Laura's eyes. "The truth."

"Do you want me to stay?"

She shook her head. "I'll do it my own way, in my own time."

Knowing she wouldn't be budged, Russ did the only thing he could do. He left.

"Is that man gone?"

Laura regarded Rufio from the doorway. His features were set in militant lines.

She nodded. Russ had been gone for at least five minutes, but she'd needed some time to compose herself and think of the right way to tell J.R. about Russ. She'd also had to dispose of the charred chicken she'd forgotten was on the grill.

"Turn off your game, *niño*. I need to talk to you."

"Mom!" he wailed. "I'm on the third level."

"Now."

Reluctantly, J.R. turned off the video game. Laura sat on the edge of his bed and patted the place beside her. Knowing he had no choice but to obey, J.R. scrambled from the floor and plopped onto the rumpled Dallas Cowboys bedspread. She scooted against the headboard and drew him onto her lap, nuzzling her lips in the softness of his bronze curls.

"I have good news and bad news."

"What's the good news?" he asked, cuddling closer.

"I burned the chicken. You get peanut butter and jelly for dinner."

Rufio tilted his head and smiled his pleasure. "What's the bad news?"

She struggled to find the right words. In spite of the changing, churning emotions instilled by Russ's visit, Laura knew she couldn't let J.R. think badly about his father.

"It really isn't bad news. I was just joking." J.R. looked at her expectantly. "Do you remember asking me about your dad?"

Rufio nodded. "You said he had a dangerous job and that he didn't want a wife and boy because he moved around a lot."

"Yes. You wanted to meet him. Do you remember that?"

J.R. nodded again. "You said you weren't sure where he was working. Maybe later, when I got older."

"That's right. Do you still want to meet him?"

Rufio leaned back in her embrace. "Can I?"

The anticipation in his eyes was promising. Maybe she could get through this without any problems, after all.

"You already have...sort of." When he frowned, she said, "The man who was here just now was James Russell Campbell. Your dad."

The expectancy on the child's face dissolved into another frown. All hope of getting through the confrontation in a calm manner vanished. He jerked free and leaped off the bed, glaring at her. "He's not my dad! He's not! He was mean to you. I don't like him. I *hate* him!''

She'd expected resistance, but the vehemence of J.R.'s outburst shocked her. ''He wasn't really being mean to me, honey, and he didn't hurt me. He was just angry about something he thinks I did.''

''I don't care! I don't want him to be my dad. I want Zach to be my dad.''

This is getting worse by the second. Laura drew in an unsteady breath. ''I know this is a surprise for you, and maybe you don't think it's a good one right now, but we can't change who our parents are. I know you love Zach, and he adores you, but he isn't your dad. He can't be.''

''He could adopt me.''

Laura's heart constricted. *Much worse.* ''You're right. He could do that,'' she said as placatingly as possible. ''But if he did, Georgia would be your mother, and you'd have to go live with them.''

J.R. thought about that a moment. ''I like Georgia, but I want you to be my mother.''

Laura's smile revealed her sorrow. ''It's a real muddle, isn't it?''

''Is he gonna move in here and sleep in your bed like Tia Inez and Tio Raul?''

The thought of Russ sharing her double bed brought a rush of memories—warm bodies tangled in sweaty sheets, hot kisses, bold male caresses.

''No! He certainly isn't. Nothing has changed, Rufio, and nothing's going to. We're going to live our lives just as we have been. I promise.''

Laura thought about her promise to J.R. long after he'd gone to bed. It was a promise she knew she couldn't keep—not if Russ decided to become a part of Rufio's life. Things had already changed. Though she knew it was silly, she already felt as if she'd given up a part of her son just because Russ knew about him.

That wasn't the only change. For years, she'd convinced herself that she was content with the status quo and happy with her life. After all, she had a beautiful son, a good job and the rare casual date. Seeing Russ made her realize how pitifully lacking her life was.

She muttered a mild curse. Why had she uncovered this unholy twin mess? Why did J.R. have to inherit a heart condition? Why couldn't she have kept him a secret forever? Even as she thought it, she knew that wasn't what she wanted.

How many times had she imagined bringing her son and his father together? How often had she dreamed the impossible dream of telling Russ about J.R. and hearing him say that he wanted them to be a real family? Despite her belief that she was a modern woman who didn't need a man to be happy, there was no denying that the fantasy held a tremendous appeal.

Because you never stopped caring for him.

The thought held her motionless, its truth paralyzing.

She'd loved Russ Campbell with all hear heart six years ago. God help her, all it had taken was one encounter with him to know she still did.

Chapter Four

Though her headache had diminished to a dull throbbing, Valerie Campbell was still cloistered in her bedroom at seven that evening. She'd presented a calm demeanor to Russ, but inside, she was furious over how such a colossal error could have been made and heartsick because she'd been denied the chance to mother her real sons.

It was appalling to think that because someone had made a mistake, she'd never laid eyes on one of her sons. God knew she loved Logan and Russ, but when she thought of Zach being raised by strangers, she wanted to cry all over again.

She'd never touched his fevered brow, never wiped his runny nose. She had no idea what kind of person he'd grown into. At least she'd had the opportunity to observe Jake's life from afar, and she'd held him in her arms and wiped his tears when Retha died, which was, perhaps, the cruelest irony of it all.

Valerie pushed the hair from her face with a trembling hand, feeling the dampness left by her tears. It wasn't fair.

But she'd learned years before that life wasn't always fair. It wasn't fair that she should have loved Jack so much when it was obvious that, even though he loved her, he loved oil more—not the money that came with bringing in a big well, but the gamble, the hard work, even the risks.

Larger than life and ornery as sin, Black Jack Campbell had cast a long shadow. She'd never met a man whose personality was strong enough to eclipse her former husband's. She often thought that he was a man born out of time, that he should have lived a hundred years earlier when the land was wild and untamed and filled with trials.

She had first met Jack when her father had hired him to work for Gaspard Enterprises. The handsome young wildcatter had seemed like a handsome god to a girl raised in a sheltered, privileged environment. Jack was well educated, and while his manners were excellent, the rough edges of his personality were as exciting as the hot looks he'd passed over her innocent body. Jack Campbell represented the two things no inexperienced girl has ever been able to resist—the forbidden and a challenge.

Why did all girls love a bad boy? Why did they think they could be the one to change him? Even after more than thirty-five years, Valerie had no answer to that question. All she knew was that the challenge of taming Jack was one she had taken on willingly. The reality was that changing that kind of man was impossible.

She knew—had known ever since the divorce—that she'd failed. Afraid of being hurt again, unwilling to throw herself into the singles arena and kissing a lot of frogs in hopes of finding a prince, she'd succumbed to the credo, "Better the devil you knew than the one you don't." She'd let the years and her life drift by, waiting for the brief interludes when she and Jack would rendezvous somewhere and indulge in a week or two of sight-seeing and sex.

She'd loved Jack, and in some ways she didn't regret her decision, but more and more the past few years, she realized that her total infatuation with him had deprived her of the love of some man who might have cherished her above everything else.

The phone rang, and Valerie grabbed the handset, grateful for a reprieve from her thoughts.

"Hello."

"Val?"

The voice was deeply masculine and familiar. A feeling of relief she wasn't aware of and couldn't begin to justify if she had recognized it, swept through her. "Ben."

"I guess Jake and Zach told you about Laura's theory," he said, getting straight to the reason for the call.

"Yes."

"How are you taking it?"

"Not well, I'm afraid," she told him in a shaky voice.

She heard him sigh. "I understand how you feel. It's been one shock after the other ever since May."

"I know," she said, realizing that he and Jake and

Zach had already been through much of what she and Logan and Russ were suffering now.

"How are Logan and Russ dealing with it?"

"Logan's doing better than Russ. He came over after the meeting this morning, and I'd say he's in complete denial, even though I told him I believed Ms. Ramirez was right."

"Damn."

"What about Jake...and Zach?" The name sounded foreign on her tongue.

"They're still in a state of shock, I think, although Jake is handling it better than I expected." Ben laughed, a bittersweet, regretful sound. "I guess after finding out after all these years that Retha and I adopted him, nothing else can come as too much of a shock."

"I suppose not."

"Look, Val, I don't mean to get in your business, but I called because it occurred to me that maybe you and the boys ought to try and get together—when you're ready."

The thought of facing two grown men, one of whom she'd thought of as a friend to her sons and the other a total stranger, was terrifying, but Valerie knew she'd taken the easy way out for too long. Besides, there was no easy way out of this.

"You're right," she said. "We need to meet and...face this."

"Would it be easier if I was there when you talk to them?"

Relief rushed through her. "You'd do that?"

"I'd be happy to, if I won't be in the way."

"Of course you won't be in the way," she scoffed. "I'd like you to be there."

"It's going to be all right, Val," Ben said. "Zach is a fine man. You'll be proud of him."

Valerie felt the threat of tears again.

"When do you want to get together? I'll have Jake fly us over in the chopper."

Her stomach churned. Panic flooded her. "Uh…I have commitments through Wednesday. I'll call you that evening and we'll set up something."

"Great. I'll tell the boys."

"I'll talk to you soon, then," Valerie said. "Good-bye." She turned the phone off and put the receiver on the bed.

She'd lied to Ben. She didn't have anything so pressing on her schedule that it couldn't be put off. But she needed the time to bolster herself for the up-coming meeting with the two men she and Jack Campbell had created through their love.

"You and Laura Ramirez have a son?" Valerie enunciated each word as if doing so was of the utmost importance in getting the facts straight. This was the last thing she'd imagined to hear when Russ invited himself over for lunch with her and Logan.

Russ tipped the dining room chair back on its flimsy legs, a habit that had often brought a lecture from her about the necessity of taking care of one's possessions. This time, she was no more aware of what he was doing than he was.

"This might not be the best time to spring it on you, with all the brouhaha over Logan and me being switched and everything, but I figured there was no sense waiting until this all died down and tossing an-other bomb into your lives."

Valerie stared at him for a few moments, then turned to Logan. "You're awfully quiet."

"Yeah, Logan," Russ mocked. "Aren't you going to tell me what an irresponsible lowlife I am for not marrying her and taking on my responsibilities?"

"I would, if I thought you'd known about it," Logan said, speaking for the first time since Russ had made the startling announcement.

Russ's heavy eyebrows drew together. "How do you know I didn't?"

"Laura told me about J.R. when Zach and Jake broke the news about us being switched."

"You knew on Saturday morning, and you didn't say anything?" Russ accused.

Logan shrugged. "She wanted to tell you and Mom in her own way. How did you find out, anyway?"

"I went to confront her about messing around in our lives, and—"

"You flew to Dallas just to chew her out for that?" Logan asked, aghast.

"Yeah."

"No," Valerie said, speaking from the thoughtful perception of a woman. "That's the reason he told himself he was going. He really went to see Laura again, didn't you, Russell? Hearing her name brought back memories, and you went to satisfy yourself that it was over."

Russ's chair crashed to the floor. Incredulous, he looked at Logan. "How does she do that?"

Logan shook his head. "Something in the feminine genes."

Shaking his head in puzzlement, Russ faced Valerie. "You're right. I wanted to see her again."

"Laura was the one you were so confused over

after the Odessa blowout, wasn't she?'' Valerie said with sudden perception.

"Yeah." Russ pushed his plate aside, leaned his elbow on the table and scraped his hand through his hair.

"And?" The question came from Valerie.

"And what?"

"What was it like, seeing her again?"

"I don't know."

"Russell…"

Russ faced his mother's query testily. He knew from experience she wouldn't stop until her maternal curiosity was satisfied. "I was angry when I got there. She tried to slam the door in my face." His attempt at a smile was more of a grimace. "It would be safe to say she wasn't particularly glad to see me."

"She was scared, most likely," Valerie said. "You can be rather intimidating."

She turned to the butler, who hovered near the kitchen door, taking in the details of the newest Campbell debacle, of which there had been more than a few. Dalton's face was expressionless. He had been with the family for thirty years, and there wasn't much he didn't know or hadn't heard. None of it surprised him after the first few months.

"We'll have our coffee and dessert in the library, Dalton."

"Yes, ma'am."

Russ and Logan followed Valerie into the leather-scented, book-lined room where she settled into a wing chair. Logan and Russ chose opposite ends of a well-used, brown leather couch.

"So tell me again how Laura came to the conclusion that we'd been switched?" Russ asked, admitting for the first time that the idea wasn't as farfetched as he'd prefer to think.

Logan went through the spiel again, finishing with, "So when Mom told her we were twins, she realized for the first time that there were *two* sets of twins born that night. At that point, anyone with two brain cells to rub together would at least toy with the possibility that a switch took place, but when Mom told her about your heart condition, that cinched it, since she'd just found out about J.R.'s heart problem."

"J.R.?" Val asked. "The boy?"

"Yeah," Russ said, his hand moving automatically to his still-sore thigh. "J.R. stands for James Russell, and believe me, the initials fit."

"And you say he has a heart condition?" Valerie asked with a hint of alarm.

"Tachycardia," Logan said. "Runaway heart rate. They just diagnosed him a week or so ago. It's controllable. He's gonna be okay. Oh, wait! I have a picture." He took the photo of J.R. from his wallet. Valerie stared at it for long seconds.

She looked slightly dazed. "I can't believe that I've gained two new sons and a grandson in the space of three days."

"J.R. isn't really your grandson," Russ reminded her.

Valerie gave a dismissive wave of her hand. Her eyes flashed with irritation. "Of course he is. Just as you and Logan are really my sons." Softness replaced the irritation in her eyes. "You don't have any idea how I've wanted one of you to get married and give me a grandchild."

"You can forget the marriage part," Russ said. "It's not gonna happen."

"What are your intentions?" Logan asked.

"I may not know who my real father is, but I don't want J.R. growing up wondering about his old man. I intend to be a part of his life," he said, his eyes blazing with determination. "No matter what Laura says."

"I want you to divorce Regina." The tone of the request sounded suspiciously like a command. It was made by the tousled, buxom blonde lying in a tangle of midnight blue satin sheets.

"Don't start, Ashlie," Tom Barnette said, shoving the tail of his shirt into his slacks. "You know my hands are tied until after the election."

"So you keep telling me," she snapped. "It's starting to sound and feel like a bad campaign promise."

His face set in angry lines, Tom turned and leaned toward her, resting his fisted hands on the bed. "Look," he said in a tone he struggled to keep calm. "I've already got more on my plate than I can handle. Regina knows I'm seeing someone, but I don't think she knows who—yet. A close source told me yesterday that there's talk that the attorney general's office is about to bring down an indictment on the Aegean Insurance deal, not to mention that I'm down in the polls. It would be nice if just once in your selfish little life, you'd think of someone besides yourself."

"You're one to talk!" Ashlie said. "Did you ever stop to think that I might like to tell someone who I'm seeing? That I might be tired of slipping around and living in constant fear that I'll say or do something to tip someone off?"

"You knew I was married when we started this," he reminded her.

"Yeah, I did. But silly me!" she said, batting her eyelashes in feigned innocence. "I thought you meant it when you said you were leaving your wife."

She rolled away from him and flounced naked from the room. The sound of the bathroom door slamming reverberated through the elegantly appointed town house, whose rent Tom paid each month.

He exhaled lustily and straightened. Lord, he thought as he zipped his pants and fastened his belt, how had he gotten himself into such a mess? He slipped on his shoes, grabbed his jacket and keys and let himself out of the apartment, knowing that the best way to handle one of Ashlie's tantrums was to leave her alone for a few days.

He wished he could disappear for a few days himself. Ashlie was getting on his nerves with her constant demands that he make an honest woman of her, and Regina's attitude was barely civil, even when they attended some civic or political function together. Women!

You'd better leave well enough alone. Caught up in the emotional chaos of the past few weeks and feeling as rudderless as a dinghy with no oars, Russ paced the small trailer he and Bliss had called home the past few years. Now parked on the Campbell Drilling yard in New Orleans, the forty-foot mobile home would soon be traded in for something newer.

His mom was going to Texas the next day, and she had asked if he and Logan wanted to join her when she met with Jake and Zach. Logan declined, stating that mountains of work had piled up while he'd tried to track down Bliss after Jack's funeral. Russ was about to say no, too, when Valerie asked if he thought it might be possible for her to meet J.R. on the neutral territory of the Lazy L.

It wasn't an unreasonable request for a grandmother. She had a right to meet J.R., just as he himself had a right to spend time with his boy. Laura wouldn't like it, though, that was a guarantee.

His jaw tightened. He didn't care what Ms. Ramirez liked. J.R. was his son, and the one thing Russ was certain about was that he wanted to be a part of J.R.'s life.

Is it J.R. you want in your life, or Laura?

The question was a valid one, one he didn't have an answer for just yet. He couldn't deny that the sight of her lush body had brought back all the old feelings of desire. When he'd had her pinned to the wall, it was all he could do to keep from kissing her senseless, all he could do to keep his hands off the tantalizing fullness of her breasts.

But it was more than that. Even in the midst of his fury and a wanting so intense he felt physical pain, he'd remembered how he'd always loved the way she looked in anger, her eyes flashing with righteous indignation, the passion that accompanied everything she undertook evident in every gesture, every word.

How could he stay mad at her for uncovering the truth when he knew that revealing truth was what drove her? How could he stay angry when that passion for fairness had been one of the things that he'd loved about her?

Russ stopped in the middle of the kitchen. *Loved?* No way. He didn't love her. The very idea was ludicrous. Impossible. Even if there was more to what he felt for her than the sex—which he wasn't ready to admit—it wasn't love. Couldn't be. Love between them would never work. They were both too hard-headed, too verbal, too volatile.

"We'd kill each other inside of six months," he said aloud, his blood quickening in his veins. It wasn't the thought of fighting to the death that stirred him. It was the image of making love to her until they were both mindless with satiation.

He wasn't aware of picking up the phone to call and accept his mother's invitation to go to Dallas until she answered the ringing.

"What are you doing here?" Laura wasn't sure which emotion had the upper hand—surprise that Russ was again standing on her doorstep, anger that he'd dared to show up unannounced, or unexpected joy at seeing him again.

To her dismay, she'd thought of little but him and their fleeting, fiery affair since he'd visited her the weekend before. Because she could barely concentrate on her job at the paper, she'd canceled interviews with the last few people who might be able to shed some light on who had fathered Logan and Russ.

Rufio had complained about her not paying any attention to him, and Inez said she had her head in the clouds. It wasn't like her to be so undisciplined.

And now, just when she'd convinced herself that she was doing better at pushing him out of her thoughts, here Russ stood in all his masculine glory, making a lie of her convictions, turning her backbone to jelly and her resolve to mush.

"I came to see J.R.," he said in answer to her question, "and to see if he can go with me out to the Lattimer ranch to meet my mother tomorrow."

Surprise robbed Laura of speech. For some reason—probably because she didn't want to deal with the accompanying complications—she'd never seriously entertained the idea that Russ would want any regular contact with J.R. Especially since their first meeting had been less than pleasant.

"Absolutely not!"

The muscle in Russ's jaw tightened. "Why?" His voice was low and pleasant. "You've met Valerie. She's a wonderful person. She was thrilled to find out she was a grandmother."

"But she isn't—not really," Laura pointed out, unwilling to concede anything that might give the Campbells the upper hand.

His wide shoulders lifted in a negligent shrug. "You try telling that to the woman who changed my diapers and doctored my skinned knees."

Laura didn't say anything. She was trying to view the situation from Valerie Campbell's point of view.

"No matter who gave birth to me, Valerie is my mother," he said, knowing as he said it that it was the one truth he could carry to his grave. "She really wants to meet J.R., and I'd like to get to know him, too."

As she considered Val's feelings, Laura felt her heart soften, but hearing Russ say he wanted to get to know Rufio hardened the protective shell again. She didn't want to set a precedent of letting Russ spend time with J.R. Doing that would only open up her heart for more pain.

"I don't think that's a good idea."

"What? Letting my son meet his grandmother or letting me get to know him?" His tone was a little louder, more aggressive, than it had been just seconds before.

"I understand where she's coming from, but I don't want Rufio's life complicated by all this."

Russ lost his tenuous hold on his composure. "Complicated!" he said loudly. "Seeing my son won't complicate his life."

Laura reacted as she'd known she would. "Just having you show up here the other day complicated his life!" she shouted. "I had to tell him that you were his father—"

"Which he had the right to know!"

"Well, it upset him. *You* upset him, barging in here and tossing your weight around," Laura cried.

"Throwing!" Russ corrected. He'd forgotten how anger sometimes caused her to revert to the word usage she'd grown up with. "*Throwing* my weight around."

The correction added fuel to her fiery fury. "Whatever!" she yelled. "He doesn't like you, so why don't you go away and let us live our lives in peace?"

She waved her hand in the air and tossed her head for emphasis. The clip holding her hair gave way, sending her haphazard hairdo tumbling.

"Fat chance," Russ snapped, but his voice was softer, his attention diverted by the torrent of dark hair that flowed in rippling waves down her back.

Seeing the dazed look in his eyes, Laura's comeback died on her lips. "What?" she asked.

"What?" he repeated, frowning as his eyes found hers.

She looked at him, really seeing him for the first time. He looked handsome and virile and totally male in faded jeans and a short-sleeve navy pullover that enhanced the musculature of his shoulders and chest.

She drew in a deep gulp of air. He was breathtaking. His auburn hair, as wavy as Rufio's, fell over his furrowed brow, and his amber eyes pierced hers with a relentless challenge she knew she had to accept.

She was suddenly aware of him not as the enemy, but as a person, a man. A man who'd once taken her to heights of pleasure. A man who'd given her a son. A son he now wanted to share.

"I want to be part of his life, Laura," he said softly, almost as if he could read her mind.

"What if I say no?"

"Then you'll be hearing from Logan."

"Logan?"

Russ nodded. "If you won't let me spend time with J.R., I'll have no choice but to pursue joint custody through the courts."

"You'd do that?" she asked as the blood drained from her head.

"In a heartbeat."

"Why?"

"Because whether or not you like it, he's as much mine as he is yours," he told her.

"This isn't about ownership, Russ."

"I know that!" He took a deep breath and put his hands on his hips. "Did you ever stop and think that there are things I might want to tell him, things I might want to do with him?"

"Like what?" she asked in a low, controlled voice.

Exasperated, he shrugged. "I don't know. Guy things."

Guilt stabbed her. Rufio had been begging all summer to go see the Rangers play. In fact, when he wasn't playing video games, he watched baseball on television.

"Have you ever taken him to see the Cowboys or the Rangers play?"

"That's low, Campbell. Even for you." Russ knew very well that she despised sports. "You know I haven't."

"What about horses? Does he like them?"

"I don't know," she said irritably. Her resolve weakened appreciably in the face of his determination and logic. "He's a city kid."

"Then why don't you let me broaden his horizons? Let me take him to the Lazy L tomorrow. My mom really wants to meet him, and he'll have fun."

Laura chewed her lower lip. "You don't know anything about taking care of little boys."

"How hard can it be?" Russ said. "I'll keep him busy. Jake has a couple of horses and a swimming pool. And Rosalita has a little girl he can play with if he gets bored with the grown-ups."

"You make a pretty strong argument," she said with a sigh, "but he's never been away for so long with someone who wasn't family."

"I'm family."

Laura looked into his eyes, trying to see past their golden highlights and into his very soul. What was he thinking? What was he really after?

"I don't have any ulterior motive," he told her, again with that uncanny ability to read her mind. "I just want to get to know him. I don't plan to kidnap him—"

She gasped.

"—or try to turn him against you. But I think he deserves a chance to get to know me and his uncle Logan and the other side of his family." Russ's grin was fleeting and sardonic. "At least as much of it as I know about."

"He may not want to go with you."

"Sure he will. I can be very persuasive."

Yes, she thought, he could. "He doesn't like you."

"The feeling's mutual," Russ said, but she saw the twinkle of mischief in his eyes and the way his hand went to his thigh.

She couldn't help smiling.

"You don't do that much, do you?" he asked.

"What?"

"Smile."

Feeling self-conscious suddenly, she pushed the hair from her face. "Sometimes when you're a single parent, there isn't a lot to smile about."

"Has it been hard?"

"Like I said, we've done better than most. It's the emotional strain that takes its toll. Like worrying about what was the matter with him when he was sick."

"I can't take away the worry, but I can promise you that you won't have to worry alone anymore."

She knew he meant the gesture to comfort her, but somehow it felt like a threat to the life she'd built so carefully. A threat to her heart. If she let Rufio go, if she gave Russ this toehold, he would bulldoze his way into their lives and turn them topsy-turvy without stopping to think about what was best for any of them. Russ always acted first, and everyone paid the consequences later.

"Well?" he asked. "Can I pick him up in the morning or not?"

"It's up to J.R.," she said, giving in to the little voice that said Russ was right to ask this of her. "Let's go see what he says."

Chapter Five

The sick feeling in Russ's stomach as he and Laura approached J.R.'s room warned him that this was the most important thing he'd ever done. Laura said J.R. was scared of him. Well, the kid might not know it, but the feeling was mutual. Whenever Russ thought about being responsible for putting J.R. in the world and how that responsibility carried over into making the child a caring, productive person—which had been often the past week—it scared him to death. Now, he prepared to face the small titian-haired boy, shaking in his shoes.

Rufio glanced up from the puzzle he was putting together. "What's he doing here?"

"He came to see if you want to go out to the country to a ranch and meet...your grandmother and uncle.

A flicker of interest briefly supplanted the antagonism in the child's eyes. "My grandmother died."

Shock sent Russ's gaze to Laura's. Her mother had died. Even though her parents lived in San Antonio, he knew she was close to them. "I'm sorry. I didn't know. When?"

"A year and a half ago," she said in an unemotional tone. "Complications from surgery."

"I'm sorry," he said again.

"So am I." She turned to Rufio. "This is another grandmother. Russ's—your...father's—mother. Her name is Valerie and she lives in New Orleans."

Another glimmer of interest flickered. "Where they have Mardi Gras?"

"Yes," Russ said, impressed by his knowledge. "If you like, I'll take you some time."

"Maybe," Rufio said, eyeing Russ reflectively. "Do I have another Gramps?"

"No," Russ said. "He died a few weeks ago. A heart—"

"Russ!" Laura interrupted, grabbing his arm and propelling him into the hallway.

"What?" he asked, frowning.

Laura tilted her head toward the bedroom. "He doesn't need to know the details," she said softly. "It might frighten him."

Russ felt as if he'd been hit between the eyes with a two-by-four. Of course he knew—now that she'd pointed it out. Rufio didn't need to hear his grandfather had died of a heart attack when he himself had just been told there was something wrong with his heart.

"I'm sorry," he said. "I wasn't thinking ahead."

"Did you ever?" she asked, turning toward the doorway.

Russ grabbed her arm. She looked at him, her full breasts rising and falling with every agitated breath she took. The scent of freesia wafted upward from her hair...or maybe her warm skin, causing a whirlwind of memories to swirl around him.

He gazed into her angry eyes. It was clear that Laura was having no similar poignant brush with the past. Instead, her eyes seemed to say, Did you ever think we might create a baby when you were making love to me twice a day?

Had he? No. They'd both been haphazard about protection. He felt inclined to tell her she was as much to blame as he was, that if she'd insisted, he'd have been more careful. But that attitude was childish, at best. Placing blame wouldn't change things, and antagonizing Laura would only hinder his attempts to get closer to J.R.

He released her arm. "Blame's easy to place, Laura, but responsibility cuts both ways."

She seemed to weigh that for a moment, and he felt a little give in the inflexibility of her stance. Taking that as a sign her mood had softened, he said, "There's more to this parenting thing than I realized."

"You have no idea."

His smile was quick, humorless. "I'm a quick study."

"You'll have to be," she said, turning and going into J.R.'s room again. "So, *niño,* do you want to go with Russ or not?"

"No. I told you I don't like him." He glared at Russ as he made the announcement.

Russ, who had adopted the sticks and stones attitude early on, had taken some verbal blows during
his life. Until now, he had no problem brushing them
off. He was surprised at how much J.R.'s opinion
stung.

Laura looked at him and gave a shrug that seemed
to say that was that. "I won't force him to go with
you."

"I don't expect you to," Russ said, his voice grating. He turned to leave the room—and the house. His
ego had taken a beating the past few minutes, and he
was smart enough to see that this whole parenting
thing was going nowhere fast. He was through the
door when J.R.'s voice stopped him.

"Do they have horses?"

Russ turned. Despite his obvious dislike for him,
J.R. was intrigued by the thought of going to the
ranch. Russ was afraid to hope the question might be
a sign the kid was changing his mind. He cast a curious glance at Laura, who stood with her arms folded
over her breasts, her full lips pressed into a tight slash
of disapproval.

He nodded. "Horses, and lots and lots of cows.
Probably some other animals, too."

"Is it a big ranch?"

"Very big. A couple of thousand acres, at least."

J.R. looked at Laura, his eyes holding a growing
excitement. "I'll bet Bobby Preston's never been to
a ranch that big, right, Mom?"

"Probably not," Laura said, clearly dismayed by
J.R.'s sudden interest.

"Who's Bobby Preston?" Russ aimed the question
at Laura.

"A kid in Rufio's kindergarten class who—if he's to be believed—has done it all."

"Ah," Russ said with an understanding nod as he advanced into the room. "His name was Clark Kennedy when I was growing up."

"Can I ride a horse?" Rufio asked eagerly. Then, as if knowing he'd given away too much, he added, "*If* I went, I mean."

"I don't ride myself," Russ said, "but Jake—the guy who owns the ranch—is a real cowboy, so I imagine a horseback ride can be arranged."

J.R.'s eyes grew wide. "A *real* cowboy? With boots and spurs and everything?"

Russ stifled a smile. "Yep. So, what do you say? Want to go with me so you can tell old Bobby what you did over the weekend?"

They watched Rufio's resolve weakening. The look Laura shot Russ told him he wasn't playing fair. The expression in his eyes said he didn't give a flying fig.

"Are you going to be mean to my mom any more?" J.R. asked, pinning Russ with a glare and getting right to the heart of the problem.

"No." Russ's answer was directed at Laura, not the child.

"Mom, are you going to yell at him?"

Conceding defeat, at least in this battle, Laura looked from Russ to the boy. "I'm certainly going to do my best not to yell at him anymore."

"Then tell each other you're sorry and kiss on the lips."

"J.R.!" Laura exploded, taking a step away from Russ as if the suggestion might cause him to pounce on her. "I don't think you're the one to be making the rules here."

"You and Tia Inez always make me and Jaunita kiss on the lips when we fight," he said.

"That's different." Darn the little brat for turning the tables on her.

"Why?"

Laura ground her teeth. Russ smiled, a wolfish smile that seemed to say that vengeance was indeed sweet. She chewed on her lower lip and glared at Russ. Rufio had her between a rock and a hard place.

Russ shrugged. "He's got a point."

"What!" Laura screeched.

"It isn't fair to expect him to live by a different code than you do." He took a step nearer her. "Come on, Laura. It's just a kiss."

Laura stared into his amber eyes, clearly horrified at the suggestion. He knew as well as she did that there was no such thing as just a kiss between them. Never had been, never would be. But aside from making a scene, there was no way she could get out of it.

He took her shoulders, kneading them lightly with his big hands. "Stop it!" she demanded in a low voice.

He pulled her closer. Laura closed her eyes and clenched her fists at her sides, trying to prepare herself for what she knew was to come.

"Look at me."

She shook her head.

He laughed, and she felt the soft burst of his minty breath against her face. "Chicken."

His lips were so close to hers she could feel them moving when he spoke. "Just do it," she said from between clenched teeth.

"With pleasure."

Though it was the briefest, softest of kisses, the touch of his mouth against hers was like being zapped by a zillion volts of electricity, or being struck by lightning, maybe. Her breath stopped. Her thought process shut down. Her toes curled in her sandals. The icy shell around her heart began to thaw, along with the center of her femininity. She realized suddenly that six years was a long time to go without loving, that she'd missed not only the man, but the kisses. The awareness of her vulnerability made her stiffen.

She felt his lips move from hers, felt his hands skim her bare arms to her hands, which he took in a loose clasp. She opened her eyes and saw in his a slumberous look she recalled all too well.

"I'm sorry," he said, his thumbs rubbing small, concentric circles on her knuckles.

He wasn't talking about their argument a week ago. He was talking about their tangled, mixed-up past. He was sorry for letting her down, letting her go.

She wanted so badly to believe him, but she'd learned her lessons from him too well. All he'd ever wanted from her was a physical relationship. That kiss—brief though it was—proved that there were plenty of embers left in the ashes of their torrid affair, enough to fan into another full-fledged conflagration...if she wanted.

Which she didn't.

She pulled her hands free, telling herself—and almost believing it—that his regrets were about six years too late.

"Are you?" she said, and slipped past him from the room.

J.R. and Laura were going with him to the Lazy L. Russ knew he should be pleased, but instead, he couldn't get past the suspicion that he was in a world of hurt. Any doubts about his feelings for her had vanished the minute he kissed her. All the old feelings were still there. He'd left her house thinking that all the cornball stuff about racing hearts and ringing bells and feet that didn't touch the ground might not be such baloney after all.

But the problem wasn't what he felt. It was how Laura felt, and it was as clear as the freckles on Rufio's face she had no desire to renew any kind of relationship with him, not even for their son's sake.

At this early stage in the game, Russ wasn't sure what he wanted from Laura, what there could be between them, but he was certain he wanted a relationship with his child. He was equally sure Laura would fight him every inch of the way...as much, he suspected, because she, too, realized there were still feelings between them as because she resented any influence he might have on J.R.

Russ didn't flatter himself that Laura had agreed to go to the ranch because of him. She was only going because J.R. requested it, and she wasn't sure about the two of them being alone together. When he thought about Rufio biting a plug out of his leg, Russ wasn't too sure about being alone with the little brat, either. The kid needed some discipline, and that was a fact.

Maybe that's why God planned for children to have two parents—not that there weren't a lot of single parents out there doing a terrific job, both male and female. But it was an inarguable fact that men and women looked at life from different perspectives and approached problems in different ways.

He knew Jack had had the devil of a time raising him and Bliss—especially Bliss—and he knew that there were times when they'd both needed nothing more than a good cry in their mothers' arms. There must have been times, too, when Logan needed a good butt kicking from Jack instead of a lecture from Valerie.

Clearly, Laura loved J.R., but it was also clear that she spoiled him. And no more than Russ had been around, he could see she was overprotective, something that seemed to go hand in hand with mothers. He was afraid that if something wasn't done to compensate, J.R. would suffer the same fate Jack Campbell had feared for his son—the life of a sissy.

Russ was well aware a person's intrinsic nature couldn't be changed, but he also knew a lot of behavior was learned. All he wanted was to be sure J.R. had a the opportunity to see both sides.

He wanted to teach him things...about oil wells and baseball and race cars. He wanted to watch him play Little League and ride a bicycle and help him with his science projects.

Surely Laura could see that J.R. was reaching an age where he needed male companionship and a strong hand. Couldn't she?

Russ, Shelby and Georgia gave Laura the grand tour of the Lazy L while Valerie met with Ben, Zach and Jake. Even though she'd known Ben and Jake for thirty-five years, Valerie wasn't sure what to expect of the meeting. It certainly wasn't to be swept into a crushing hug by Jake, who whispered fiercely, "Hi, Mom."

Valerie clung to him tightly, not even trying to halt

the tears that ran down her cheeks, splotching her makeup and smearing her mascara. Finally, when she thought her legs could hold her, she pressed a kiss to Jake's cheek and stepped away.

"I always was inordinately fond of you," she said with an unsteady smile.

"I was you, too," Jake said, grinning at her. Funny, she thought with a little catch in her breath. Why had she never noticed before how much like Jack Jake looked when he smiled?

Jake stepped back and gestured toward the man standing near the window, an uncertain look on his face. Without hesitating, Valerie crossed the room to stand before her other son. The look in his eyes was guarded, unsure. On the outside, he was identical to Jake. But inside, he was different. She knew that from talking to Ben.

She felt the tears start again, and again she found no strength or need to stop them. It wasn't fair that she should have been denied watching Zach and Jake grow up together.

"Zach," she said, holding out her hands, uncertain if he would accept an embrace from her. Her smile felt as shaky as her legs and her voice.

He reached for her hands. Unlike the look in his eyes, his grip was firm, sure. She couldn't think of anything to say except, "I can't believe how much you look like Jake...and your father."

Incredibly, the mundane observation brought a smile to Zach's shapely mouth. Jack's mouth. Jack's smile.

"And I can't believe how beautiful you are," he replied.

Valerie made a sound that was something between

a laugh and a sob. She turned to look at Ben and Jake, who stood by the doorway, watching. "Oh, he's definitely Jack's son."

"I told you," Ben said with a smile.

Valerie looked at Zach, the yearning in her heart shining through her tear-glazed eyes. "I'm concerned about a matter of protocol, here."

"What's that?" he asked.

"Do Texas Rangers hug their mothers?"

"Only if their mother wants them to," Zach said solemnly.

"She does."

The next thing Valerie knew, she was being held close again, and again she gave in to the pain of her loss. Finally, remembering how much Jack had hated her woman's tears, she struggled to get herself under control. When she stepped back, she cradled Zach's face between her palms. "I'm so sorry that I wasn't there for you and Jake."

"We don't need to think about that," Zach said, his voice suspiciously gruff. "It was beyond your control. We should just be glad we finally found each other."

She nodded and wiped her eyes with the tissue clutched in her hand. "You're right. I guess the thing to do is be thankful I can be a mother to four wonderful sons instead of two."

"Yeah," Jake said, "Zach and I have talked, and we don't want Logan and Russ to think anything is going to change. It may sound corny, but we hope we can all be just one big happy family."

"It doesn't sound corny to me," Valerie said. "It sounds pretty wonderful."

"To me, too," Ben said, his voice gruff with emotion.

"Speaking of Russ and Logan, is Laura any nearer finding out who their father is?"

Ben shook his head. "She talked to a nurse friend of Lillian's and to an old boyfriend of Abby's, but nothing came of it. She had a few more leads, but she's been too worried about J.R. and too busy interviewing for that television position to follow up on them."

Valerie's face brightened at the mention of J.R. "He's a doll, isn't he?"

"Cute as a button," Ben agreed.

"Ornery as sin," Zach said.

Valerie laughed. "I heard about him biting Russ on the leg."

"That sounds like Rufio," Zach said with a nod. "What he needs is a firm hand."

"Which brings me to the next question," Jake said. "What do you think will happen with Russ and Laura?"

"Who knows?" Valerie said, shaking her head. "I think Russ still cares for her. Actually, I'm not sure he realized it until he saw her again. But whether or not they can work through whatever problems they had in the past—or even if they want to—remains to be seen."

"At least you have your first grandchild," Ben said.

"But not your last," Jake offered.

"I certainly hope not," Valerie replied.

"Definitely not your last."

"Are you trying to tell us something, hoss?" Zach asked his sibling.

"Tell 'em, Jake," Ben urged, smiling broadly.

Jake's smile was wide and proud. "Shelby and I are going to have a baby in the spring."

The announcement brought another rush of tears to Valerie's eyes.

"What's the matter, Val?" Ben asked, slipping a comforting arm around her shoulders and pulling her against his side. "That's good news, isn't it?"

"Nothing's wrong, and yes, it's wonderful news," she said, smiling at him through her tears. "I'm just very, very happy."

What on earth was she doing here? Laura accepted a cup of coffee from Rosalita and joined Shelby and Georgia as they meandered toward the barn where Leza and Rufio were headed to see the kittens.

She didn't blame J.R. for not wanting to be alone with Russ. He was a stranger, after all. Nor could she blame him for wanting to take Russ up on his offer. The picture he'd painted of the ranch and the animals and all the things J.R. could do had been enough to make her envious of the opportunity to get away from the crazy pace of the city. Maybe that's why she'd jumped at the chance to tag along when Rufio had turned his pitiful gaze on her and begged her, "Please come too, Mom."

But the little voice in the back of Laura's mind whispered that even though it was insane and she'd pay for the foolishness later, her decision had a lot more to do with the kiss she and Russ had shared than Rufio's pleading.

"He and Leza are getting along great, aren't they?" Georgia said, pushing her sunshades up on her nose.

"Yes, they are." Laura agreed, glad for the interruption of her thoughts. J.R. and Leza had hit it off from the moment Ben introduced them.

"Leza is happy to have some company," Shelby said. "She gets lonely out here with just us grownups."

Laura had been dubious about how Rufio would react to meeting so many people, but he'd done her proud, extending his hand whenever he was introduced to an adult and letting Valerie hug him with no complaint. So far, he'd been on his best behavior. But, she thought, watching him follow Leza into the barn, the day was young.

Still, even if he did commit some serious social faux pas, there was no denying the outing was agreeing with him. It did Laura's heart good to see the color in his cheeks, to see him laughing and running after he'd spent so much time lying around the house.

"I've been telling Rosalita for a couple of years that she and Ernesto need to have another baby," Georgia said. "But she wanted to get her teaching degree first. I'm afraid the age gap between Leza and a new baby will be too great for them to be really close if Rosie waits too much longer."

A wave of panic washed over Laura. Leza and Rufio were about the same age. Had she waited too long to have another baby? She'd been too busy getting over Russ Campbell, pursuing a career and planning for the future to take time out for more than superficial personal relationships. Had her single-minded determination to make it on her own cheated her son of the pleasures of a brother or sister?

"Well, speaking of babies," Shelby said, interrupting the disquieting turn of Laura's thoughts,

"Jake and I are having one. Or we think it's only one at this point."

Laura's quandary vanished. Almost simultaneously with Georgia, she squealed and flung her arms around Shelby's neck. Though Shelby's nature had kept them from becoming really close friends, Laura had known Shelby for a long time. Zach had told Laura some of Shelby's background, and if anyone deserved love and happiness, she did.

"Oh, Shelby! I'm so thrilled!" Georgia said, tears in her eyes. "When's it due?"

"Sooner than it ought to be," Shelby said, her face turning a becoming pink. "Must have been those moonlight rides."

Laura didn't ever remember seeing the tough former cop blush.

"What does Jake think?"

Shelby rolled her eyes and hooked her thumbs in the front pockets of her jeans. "You'd think he was the only man to ever father a child. He's taking such good care of me, he's about to drive me crazy. And if he's bad, Ben's worse."

Laura and Georgia laughed.

"How about you?" Laura asked. "How do you feel about becoming a mother?"

Tears sprang into Shelby's eyes. "I guess awe pretty much describes it. To think that through our love Jake and I have created another human life is almost more than I can comprehend. And when I think of the responsibility involved in bringing up a child... It's pretty heavy stuff, you know?" She swiped at her eyes. "Sorry about that. I tend to be a little emotional these days."

"I cried buckets of tears when I was pregnant with

J.R.,'' Laura said. "My hormones were a mess." She looked around. "I wonder where J.R. is?"

"He's around somewhere. He can't hurt anything," Shelby said.

Laura gave her a you've-got-to-be-kidding-me look.

"Speaking of messed-up hormones, I was talking to my friends Ruthie and Myra the other day—they're a couple of sweet little old ladies I met at the airport the day I found Zach. We've kept in touch."

When the explanation made Laura look even more puzzled, Georgia grinned and pinned her with a look of mock reproach. "What's the matter, Laura? You didn't make the logical, connecting leap with me?"

Laura, whose mind was still troubled over the possibility that she'd waited too long to have another baby, said, "No, I'm sorry."

"Just teasing. There's no way you could. My mind is always half a dozen steps ahead of the conversation. I make these mental connections and blurt out something that makes sense to me but leaves everyone else scratching their heads."

Laura nodded, wishing Georgia would get to the point and wondering where J.R. was and what he was into. "So what do these old ladies have to do with messed-up hormones?"

"Whatever she says, don't laugh," Shelby cautioned. "Her mind takes some pretty strange leaps. She'd have been a great cop."

"Thanks," Georgia said with a smile. "It seems Ruthie used to work at a home for unwed mothers. Get it? Overactive hormones?"

Laura forced a smiled. "Got it."

"She said she'd be glad to talk to you."

"I appreciate that, but I pretty well have all the information I need for the article."

"Oh. Okay. I'll tell her," Georgia said with a shrug. "Oh, look! There's J.R. He's *so* cute!"

J.R. came out of the barn with a kitten tucked under each arm. A huge ratty-looking black cat followed.

"Good grief!" Laura said, the conversation about Georgia's friend Ruthie forgotten. "That looks like Attila."

"It is," Shelby said.

"How did he get out here?"

"He stowed away with Jake one day when he'd been to Zach's apartment."

"He's the father of these kittens?"

"Unfortunately," Shelby said with a sardonic smile. "Jake said he thought Elizabeth had higher standards than to be wooed by a devil like Attila, but I reminded him that most women are a sucker for a bad boy." Her smile broadened. "I guess that applies to lady felines, too."

It certainly applied to her, Laura thought.

"Hey." Shelby cried, a wicked gleam in her eyes. "I've got an idea. How about letting J.R. take home a kitten?"

"No, thanks," Laura said, "but I can guarantee J.R. will ask for one before we leave."

"Gives me time to try and soften you up," Shelby said, smiling. "And if I haven't said so, I'm really glad you came."

She leaned against the board fence, hooking the heel of her boot on the bottom board and her elbows on another. "I love it out here, but I get lonesome for old friends sometimes."

"Thanks," Laura said, "but I probably wouldn't have come if Rufio hadn't insisted."

"I don't mean to pry, but if there's anything you'd like to tell us about J.R. and Russ, we'll be glad to listen," Shelby offered. "You've certainly kept it in a long time."

"I don't think you're prying," Laura said, "but there isn't much to tell. What you said about Elizabeth and Attila pretty well sums it up. Nice girl falls for bad boy and realizes too late she can't change him."

"Zach says you'd have kept J.R. a secret forever if his heart problem hadn't shown up," Georgia said.

Laura shrugged. "Maybe I would have. I don't know. Telling everyone who his father was wouldn't have changed things."

"So where do the two of you go from here?"

"It looks like I let Russ take part in J.R.'s life whether I like it or not." She didn't tell the other two women she was afraid that if Russ decided he wanted J.R. the Campbells had the money and the power to take him from her.

"Why is that a problem?" Georgia asked. "It seems to me that having someone to share the responsibility of raising J.R. would take a big burden off you."

"It's because you're still crazy about the big idiot, isn't it?" Shelby asked, a sly smile on her angular face.

Air whooshed from Laura's lungs in a deep sigh of defeat. "No," she said, the anger in her voice as much to convince herself as her friends. "I'm not."

"Well, that's too bad," Shelby said. "Because I was watching Russ earlier, and he looked like he wanted to drag you off to the bushes somewhere and ravish you.''

As Shelby's had earlier, Laura's face flamed with color. "There was never anything wrong with our physical relationship," she admitted with an honesty that surprised her. "But Russ was never strong into things like commitment and forever."

"That was then," Shelby said cryptically. "This is now."

"Shelby's right," Georgia added. "He's changed. I haven't seen a lot of him through the years, but I have seen him do a lot of growing up. Maybe it took losing you to make him realize that his priorities were all messed up."

"I appreciate the sentiment," Laura said, "but just because the two of you have found your man and Logan and Bliss are getting married doesn't mean Russ is ready to settle down with a wife and child."

"It still might be worth exploring," Georgia said.

Laura shook her head. "Being a dad and being a husband are two entirely separate things. Russ can be Rufio's dad when it's convenient for him. Committing to a relationship with a woman is something altogether different, and I haven't seen anything to make me think he's ready for that—even if *I* was, which I'm certainly not. Not with him, anyway."

"Methinks the lady reporter protests too much," Shelby misquoted with a conspiratorial wink at Georgia.

"Me, too, Shel," Georgia said with a grin. "And I oughta know, 'cause I been there and done that."

"Haven't we all," Shelby said with a short laugh. "And just look at us now."

"Yeah, look at us."

"Mom?"

The sound of Rufio's excited voice interrupted the feminine conversation. Laura turned with a smile. "What is it, *niño?*"

The look on his face was intent, the expression in his eyes pleading. "Leza said they had too many cats. Can I have one?"

"No, Rufio."

"Please?" he begged, his little face drawn into lines of pleading.

Georgia and Shelby burst into laughter. Laura looked at Shelby with an I-told-you-so smile. "What did I tell you?"

"Please, Mom!"

"No, Rufio. Having a pet is a big responsibility, and I don't have the time."

"I'll feed him, I promise. And I'll take him outside to go to the bathroom."

"You don't take cats outside. They have a litter box that has to be cleaned every day," she explained.

"I'll clean it, then." He sketched a quick X over his heart. "Cross my heart and hope to die," he said, jumping up and down.

"What's the problem?"

The trio of women turned at the sound of Russ's voice. Noticing that her heart began beating a little faster, Laura tried to control the expression on her face.

"No problem," she said. "J.R. wants to take a kitten home."

"And I suppose that's out of the question," he said, his unusual amber-colored gaze probing hers.

"Yes." Laura made her voice firm, the look in her

dark eyes decisive. "He's too young for the responsibility."

Russ nodded. "I can certainly relate to that."

Laura wondered if the other two women read the undertones of his statement.

"Look, J.R.," Russ said, squatting on his haunches in front of the boy, "maybe it isn't a good time to get a pet. Your mom has a lot on her mind right now with all your tests and her job interviews and everything. It wouldn't be fair to the kitten if you forgot to feed it and your mom was too busy."

J.R. stuck out his lip.

"Maybe later, huh, Mom?" Russ asked as they both cast a hopeful look toward Laura.

Laura felt herself softening. How could she deny them anything? The only time she'd ever denied Russ was when he'd suggested she follow him from well site to well site. She sighed. He was playing on her sympathy, but she supposed she should be glad he hadn't overridden her veto altogether.

"Maybe," she hedged. *A lot later*.

"See?" Russ said to Rufio. The boy still didn't look too pleased, but his frown vanished. Russ stood. "I came to tell you Ben is getting ready to put the hamburgers on the grill."

"Good," Shelby said. "I'm starving."

Russ threw a companionable arm around her shoulders. "Yeah," he said with that devastating grin, "I hear you're eating for two."

"Yep," she said, sliding her arm around his waist as if they were old friends instead of two people who'd just met a few hours ago.

Russ—the eternal flirt. As for Shelby, well, there was no doubt she was head over heels in love with

Jake, and Laura supposed her friend's ease with Russ had a lot to do with the fact that she'd worked so closely with men in the past.

Even so, Laura couldn't help the knife of jealousy twisting in her heart, tangible proof that her feelings for him were more involved than she'd like to believe.

She sighed. "Come on, Rufio," she said to the boy watching Russ with a considering gleam in his eyes. "Let's eat."

Chapter Six

For lunch, they ate a huge batch of homemade French fries and a platter of hamburgers made from Lazy L beef, along with more toppings than a gourmet burger joint. The only jarring incident was when J.R. took aim with a squirt bottle and zapped Leza with a stream of catsup.

Horrified, Laura snatched the laughing J.R. and marched him into the house while Rosalita bustled the wailing Leza inside for a bath. When both children returned, J.R., who looked sufficiently chastised and at least momentarily contrite, was made to sit next to his red-faced mother. Leza, clearly wary of her new friend, stayed close to a tight-lipped Rosie.

When they finished the meal, a more subdued affair since the catsup attack, Rosalita brought out a pan of brownies topped with swirls of gooey fudge icing and marshmallow cream. They were delicious, but the adults couldn't enjoy theirs to the fullest, since part of J.R.'s punishment was to forgo dessert.

As soon as was socially acceptable, Ben and Valerie escaped to take a walk to "let their lunch settle."

Shelby wanted to take Georgia and Laura inside to show them the newest acquisition to the doll collection that had once belonged to Jake's mother. The porcelain and leather doll was a genuine Bru *bébé* Ben had bought for her from an estate auction when he'd flown to France to take a look at a champion Charolais bull. Seeing the trepidation in Laura's eyes at the thought of J.R. in a room with a priceless doll collection, Russ volunteered to watch their son while Laura joined the ladies.

While the girls were oohing and ahing over the baby doll, and Shelby tried to recover from her shock when Georgia told her how many thousands of dollars Ben must have paid for it, J.R. sat alone at Leza's miniature table, which was all set up for a tea party, complete with cherry Kool-Aid in the teapot and tiny brownies on a floral-bordered plate.

Unfortunately, the hostess had abdicated. Leza wanted nothing to do with her guest. Which served the little urchin right, Russ thought. It would be good for J.R. to stew in his own juices for a while.

Zach and Jake each commandeered a lounge chair near the pool and stretched out in the warm October sun, carrying on a desultory conversation and fighting off sleep.

Feeling the weight of his meal taking its toll, Russ wanted nothing more than to join them. Instead, he went over and squatted beside J.R., fully prepared to feel the brunt of the boy's hostility, which was never far from the surface whenever Russ came around.

"Rosalita said it was okay if you have a party by yourself. The dolls are here, and the cats."

The children had carried two of the kittens from the barn to attend their afternoon soirée. Their party clothes—doll dresses and bonnets—lay on one of the miniature chairs.

"I don't want to," J.R. said, his bottom lip protruding in a way that was becoming familiar to Russ. "Tea parties are sissy stuff, anyway."

"On the contrary," Russ said, leaning against the side of the house and wrapping his arms around his knees, "kids' tea parties are a sort of…social function that will get you ready to face the grown-up world."

J.R.'s gaze moved from the playing kittens to Russ. "What's a social function?"

The question caught Russ off guard. "It's an activity where a lot of people who are sometimes very different get together to talk, like all of us getting together here."

"What do they talk about?"

Jeez, the kid was full of questions! "Sometimes important things that have to do with work, sometimes just everyday stuff, like, How's it going at work, Bob? How are the kids, Ralph? Did you see the ball game last night, J.R.? That sort of stuff."

Instead of coming back with another question, J.R. said. "Yeah, I saw it. The Rangers lost."

The unexpected comment surprised Russ as much as J.R.'s questions. "Yeah, they did. They're out of the play-offs. You like baseball, huh?"

J.R. looked at Russ and nodded. "I like football, too, but not as much as baseball."

"Have you ever been to a game?"

J.R. glanced away. "No. My mom doesn't like sports."

"Well, I do. Would you like to come to New Orleans and go to a Saints game sometime?"

J.R. found Russ's gaze again. Excitement sparked in the depths of his eyes. He banked it quickly. "I don't know. Maybe."

"Your mom could come, too. You could fly over and spend the whole weekend."

"Fly? In a real airplane?" J.R. asked, unable to hide his excitement.

Russ smiled at him. "Yeah, in a real airplane, unless you got wings under that shirt."

J.R. shook his head. The briefest smile flickered across his lips as he said, "Nah." His eyes held a faraway look as he repeated reverently, "Wow. A real airplane."

Seeing that he was making headway, Russ pressed on. "Bliss could fly you and your mom over and you could stay with your grandma Valerie and meet your uncle Logan."

"Who's Bliss?"

"Bliss is the pretty lady who is going to be your aunt. She's a pilot."

"Wow!"

The thought of the unconventional Bliss hooking up with the ornery J.R. was enough to bring a shiver of apprehension and a smile of delight. "You'll like Bliss," Russ said. "She sometimes does unexpected things at social functions, too. And she has her own plane, so she can take you up any time."

If J.R.'s eyes got any wider, they'd pop out of his head. Russ stifled a grin. "You think about that."

He waited a few seconds and said, "You know,

it's really important to behave correctly when you go somewhere. Sometimes when Bliss shows up at a party and she isn't dressed right, people talk about her, which isn't good. You need to be on your best behavior, because you want people to always have good stuff to say about you.''

Russ heard the words coming from his mouth and remembered all the things he'd done in the past. He felt like a hypocrite, preaching mores to J.R., but thanks to his mom's teachings and a healthy fear of Jack's belt, his shenanigans hadn't thrown the family name in a bad light. The Campbells were big on keeping the name unsullied.

J.R. sighed in resignation. ''That's what my mom says. She wants people to think I'm a good boy so they'll want me to come back. She says if I'm bad, it's a 'flection on her and people might think she's a bad mom.''

''She's right. And you wouldn't want that, would you?''

J.R. shook his head. ''We don't ever go to any social auctions.''

''No?'' Russ asked, hiding his laughter behind his hand and a cough. When he got himself under control he said, ''Well, you might go to a lot of them one day. You'll own part of Grandma Val's company when you're older, and part of Campbell Drilling. Or,'' he added thoughtfully, ''you might decide to be a lawyer like your uncle Logan. Lawyers go to lots of social functions.''

''Are you a lawyer?''

Russ shook his head. ''I drill oil wells.''

''Cool,'' J.R. said, the interest back in his amber-hued eyes. "Does it really squirt up out of the ground like I've seen on TV?"

"Sometimes," Russ said.

"I'll bet you get really dirty," J.R. said longingly.

"Really dirty," Russ said with a nod. "Maybe you could come to a site sometime."

Again, J.R. chose to play coy. "Maybe."

"What do you want to be when you grow up?"

"A pitcher for the Braves," J.R. said. "But I didn't get to play T-ball this year because I was sick, and Mom said she didn't think I could next year, either, because I've got something wrong with my heart." He gave a heavy sigh. "She won't let me do anything but play stupid video games."

"I had something wrong with my heart when I was a kid, too," Russ said, stretching out his legs.

"Really?"

Russ nodded. "But I outgrew it. Maybe you'll outgrow yours, too."

"I hope so. 'Cause I really, really want to play ball."

The ache constricting Russ's heart was unexpected and painful. He and Laura needed to have a serious talk about J.R.—the sooner the better.

He pushed away from the wall of the house and stood up. "Want to take a nap?"

J.R. looked shocked by the very thought. "Do you?"

"Yeah. It's one of those strange things that happen when you get older," Russ told him. "You start wanting to take naps."

"Not me," J.R. said.

Russ sighed, visions of catching forty winks disappearing like pipe down a drilling hole. "Fine. I'll just sit in that other lounge chair and watch while you play with the kitten, okay?''

"Okay.''

Russ took the lounger between his friends, who had already succumbed to the somnolence induced by the warmth of the sun and the meal they'd just eaten, and crossed his arms over his chest, watching as Attila crossed the cool deck and crawled into J.R.'s lap. He began scratching the huge tom behind the ears. Russ heard the cat's deep, satisfied rumbling from where he sat. He smiled. *Soul mates.*

There was something mesmerizing about the sound of Attila's purring and the soft whirring and irritated chitter of the dozens of hummingbirds that vied for a place at the feeders Rosalita kept filled. Russ closed his eyes.

He heard J.R.'s giggles, Zach's soft snoring and the faraway lowing of cattle. The faint scent of chlorine filled his nostrils reminding him of another time, another pool. A time Laura's kisses had awakened him....

Something was tickling his chest. He ought to brush it away, but there was something seductive about the feeling, something that roused him sexually. The feather-light touches moved up, stirring his chest hair, brushing his nipples...gliding up to whisper against his chin, his cheek and his eyes before finally settling with exquisite gentleness on his lips.

Laura.

The very thought of her name filled him with pleasure and a rising excitement. He forced his eyelids upward and saw her leaning over him, a hot look of passion in her eyes.

He reached up and worked his fingers in the knot atop her head, pulling the pins from her hair so that the dark mass tumbled around her face. Her breath caught in her throat, a soft sob of need that was echoed by the heat in her eyes. He felt his libido kick into overdrive.

Tangling his fingers in her hair, he dragged her mouth to his, kissing her over and over. Like his, her mouth was open, hungry, matching the darting forays of his tongue with those of her own, nipping, tasting, teasing. She pulled back, panting slightly.

"Russ," she said. "Not here."

He remembered then that they were in the motel swimming area. It was night, the small motel was barely half full, and those who were staying there were occupied somewhere else.

Russ got to his feet, swept her into his arms and carried her to the hot tub that was situated at the end of the pool where, thankfully, the bulb of the nightlight needed replacing. The hot tub nestled in the shadows, lit only by the low-voltage beams of the pool lights.

"Russ, no."

"Yes." He sank into the water and pulled her onto his lap, facing him, pressing her against the strength of his need. She sucked in a little breath, and he took the opportunity to kiss her, stealing her lips and her breath. He threaded his fingers through her hair, holding her lips captive to his.

Hot water swirled and pulsed around them, an elusive, erotic caress. The receptive capabilities of every nerve ending seemed enhanced. It seemed he could feel where each individual hair grew from her scalp. He tasted not only her mouthwash, but the perfume of the lip gloss slicking her mouth. The fragrance of her—her hair, her cologne…the unique smell of her heated skin filled his nostrils, his lungs, his soul, branding him with the essence of her as surely as if she'd seared his heart with a red-hot iron.

She moved against him, no longer unwilling but eager, needing, as hungry as he. Without taking his lips from hers, he half lifted her, and made some adjustments to their clothing.

She sucked in a soft hiss of air. Russ marveled at the perfection of it, at the way she moved in absolute sync with him. At the way their hearts beat as one. At the joy flooding him…

Far, far too soon, their soft cries of fulfillment spilled into the night. Neither of them thought about the protection in the motel room. Neither thought.…

A splash and a blood-curdling scream brought Russ to rude wakefulness. He bolted upright, along with Zach and Jake. Russ spared a quick look at Leza's table and saw Attila smack dab in the middle, nipping daintily at a brownie. He didn't see J.R. anywhere.

"In the pool!"

The sound of Jake's voice galvanized Russ into action. He was kicking off his shoes even as his head whipped toward the sounds of splashing at the pool's deep end. J.R. floundered near the edge. Panic bolted through Russ like a surge of electricity. If anything happened to the kid, Laura would never forgive him.

He'd never forgive himself.

He made a shallow dive into the pool and swam toward J.R., coming up beneath him, looping an arm around his slender body. A strong kick of Russ's legs sent them shooting to the surface, where Jake and Zach waited.

Jake grabbed J.R. under the arms and hauled him to safety. Zach gave Russ a hand out. He slicked his wet hair from his forehead and snatched J.R. out of Jake's arms, holding his wet, squirming body close and breathing a prayer of thankfulness.

J.R. laughed. "You swim pretty good."

Expecting choking and coughing, Russ drew back, shocked by the observation. J.R. grinned at him, mischief gleaming in his eyes.

"What on earth happened?"

Russ turned toward the worried sound of Laura's voice. He set J.R. down, and the boy raced toward his mother.

"J.R. fell into the pool."

Surprisingly, Laura's worry seemed to vanish. She grasped the boy's chin and tilted his face so she could look at him. She seemed more exasperated than scared. "What on earth were you doing, *niño?*"

"The hummingbird feeder was empty," he said, pointing to the feeder that hung, along with several plants, from a decorative wrought-iron pole set in concrete near the edge of the pool.

"I was going to put some Kool-Aid in there for the birds, but my chair tipped over and I fell in."

Laura placed her hands on her hips. "Hummingbirds shouldn't drink Kool-Aid."

"It was red, so I thought it would be okay," J.R. said in self-defense.

Laura turned to Russ, accusation in her eyes. "Where were you?"

He felt his face flame. "I...guess I dozed off for a

minute. I take full responsibility. If anything had happened to him, I'd never forgive myself."

"Me, either," Laura said, her eyes cool.

"Mom," J.R. said, "I was okay. I just yelled because I was surprised." He looked at Russ.

"You were fine?" Russ asked.

"Yeah." J.R. grinned. "I was a water baby. I've been swimming all my life."

"How did the weekend go?" Logan asked his mother and brother on Monday morning. After returning from Dallas on Sunday evening, Russ elected to stay overnight at the Gaspard mansion instead of going to his lonely trailer.

"It was wonderful," Valerie said, filling a delicate china cup with coffee and joining her two sons at the table. "Jake and Zach were very...accepting."

"That's good." Logan popped a bite of English muffin into his mouth. His smile was indulgent, curious. "And how was your new grandson?"

"Adorable. He didn't have a lot to do with me. He was too busy having fun."

"He's a menace to society," Russ growled. "He squirted catsup in Leza's hair and fell into the pool trying to feed the hummingbirds Kool-Aid."

Logan laughed.

"Rub it in if you want," Russ said, "but it scared me out of a year's growth. I jumped in after him, thinking he was drowning, and find out after my daring rescue the little brat can swim like a fish."

"Couldn't you see he wasn't struggling?" Logan asked, his eyes dancing with mirth.

"I was too busy acting the role of a panicked parent to notice details like that."

"Well, I say it serves you right for all the scares you gave me and Jack," Valerie said.

"*Et tu*, Mom?" Russ said, placing a hand over his heart as if he'd just taken a knife thrust.

"This is good for you," she said, patting his hand. "You know what they say about paying for your raising. Just think of these little episodes with J.R. as character-building experiences."

Russ muttered something under his breath his mother and brother couldn't make out. They exchanged amused glances.

"By the way, Logan," Valerie said, "I'm going to have another grandbaby. Did Russ tell you?"

"Russ, you dog!" Logan said, giving his brother a deliberate dig.

Russ held his palms out. "It's not me. The way my love life has been the past year, I could qualify for sainthood."

Logan laughed. "Whoa! Too much information." He turned to his mother. "Who's the lucky couple?"

"Jake and Shelby," Valerie said. She scooted back her empty plate and rested her arms on the table, leaning forward eagerly. "You should see them together, Logan. Jake is so tender with her, and she's crazy about him. It does my heart good to see him so happy. I always loved Georgia, and I admit I was a little miffed at her when she left Jake at the altar, but now that I see how right she is for Zach, and how perfect Jake and Shelby are together, all I can think is thank God she came to her senses in time."

"I'm glad it all worked out and Jake and Zach have made their peace," Logan said.

"Me, too."

"Speaking of working things out, when is your former sparring partner and newly betrothed coming home?'' Russ asked, slathering butter on an English muffin.

Logan set his cup in its saucer. "She called last night. She's flying in this evening."

"I've missed her," Valerie said. "It's been nice having another woman around the past few weeks."

"She misses you, too," Logan said. "And she can't wait to show you her wedding gown. She swears she bought the most gorgeous dress on the continent, and if the price is any indication, she's probably right."

Valerie made a little moue of irritation. "You aren't paying for it, so stop acting like an old Scrooge. Who's the designer?"

"Jessica McClintock."

"Mmm," Valerie purred appreciatively. "Pure class."

Russ snorted and got up to fill his plate from the covered dishes residing on the kidney-shaped buffet that had been handed down from Valerie's mother.

"Personally," he said, "it's hard to connect *class* and Baby Sister in the same thought. I can't picture her in anything but ragged jeans, a tank top and a pair of worn-out boots."

Logan's smile was fond, indulgent. "That's the real Bliss, all right, but she does clean up nicely. She'll make a good lawyer's wife."

Russ laughed and speared a fork full of ham and cheese frittata. "Speaking of lawyers, what have you heard from the attorney general?"

"Russ, don't get him started," Valerie chided, knowing that once Logan began talking about his nemesis, Tom Barnette, their pleasant breakfast conversation would come to an end.

"Nothing. I don't know if the witness backed out or if someone dropped the ball after I handed over my information."

"You're just too impatient, dear," Valerie told him. "This isn't the sort of thing you want to go off half-cocked on." She stood. "Russell, would you like some more coffee?" The look in her eyes begged him to try to divert his brother's attention.

"Sure. Thanks, Mom."

Logan saw the wordless communication and took the hint. "I don't suppose Laura has found out anything else about our paternity."

Russ shook his head. "She talked with one of Abby's old boyfriends, but he swears he never touched her, and Laura believes him. She has a couple more interviews with some of Abby's schoolmates, but if those don't turn up something new, she's out of leads."

"It's hell, isn't it?" Logan asked thoughtfully. "To have everything you believe about yourself yanked out from under you, so to speak. The hardest part for me isn't accepting that Abby Pickett is our real mother. It's not knowing anything about our dad."

Russ nodded. "There was a certain security in knowing I was Valerie and Jack Campbell's son, knowing I was grounded in that rich Irish and Creole heritage. That's the hell of it. Not having any roots."

"You have roots," Valerie said, setting the coffee cups on the table. "Jack and I gave them to you. I know it's hard, but both of you will get past this."

"Yeah, I guess so."

"So," she said, injecting a deliberately light tone

into her voice and deftly changing the subject, "what does Bliss plan to do with herself once you're married?" Valerie asked Logan. "The two of you have been pretty closemouthed about your plans."

"Well, she sure as heck isn't going to spend her days going to lunches and garden club meetings," Russ drawled. "I can promise you that."

"You're right," Logan said. "Actually, she's going into the charter business with a friend."

Valerie's eyebrows rose in delicate dual arches. "Really? Who?"

"Remember Buzz Anderson?"

"Isn't he the big guy with the crew cut and tattoo who helped with the search when you and Bliss crashed in Big Bend?" Valerie asked.

"The same."

She propped her chin in her hand. "And how do you feel about that?"

Logan raised his eyebrows. "How do I feel about that? Hmm," he said thoughtfully. "Thankful Buzz doesn't look like Tom Cruise. Other than that, I'm fine with it. Russ is right. Bliss would never be content to be a typical lawyer's wife...if there is such a thing."

"Have you found a house yet?" Russ asked.

"Actually, we're going to take Mom up on her offer to stay here when we're in the city."

"You're thinking of moving?" Russ asked, shocked by the idea.

"Not moving, exactly, but I am planning on turning over some of my workload for Gaspard Enterprises to Cousin Emile. He's smart, honest and eager to prove himself."

"Sounds like a good move. What about Campbell Drilling?" Russ asked with concern.

"The oil operation isn't as intricate as the Gaspard holdings, so I'll keep doing all that myself."

"I think what I'm hearing is that you want to spend some time with your new wife," Valerie said, smiling her approval.

"Exactly. I'm thirty-five. I've waited a long time for the right woman. I don't want to lose her because I'm so tied up with my work that she feels like low guy on the totem pole."

"Been there, done that," Valerie quipped.

"You have, haven't you?" Russ said, recalling the nights he'd lain awake and listened to her and his dad argue about the time he spent away from home. "You wasted a lot of years just being there for Dad when he wanted you."

"I did, didn't I?" Her smile was bittersweet. "But I made my choice, and I have no regrets." Her laugh was brief and a bit brittle. "Well, not many, anyway."

"You're still a beautiful woman, Mom," Logan told her. "There's no reason you can't find some good man and get married again. As a matter of fact, until Russ told me about your and Dad's clandestine little affair, I always wondered why you hadn't remarried."

Valerie laughed. "I'm not opposed to marrying again. Find me a good man, and I'll think about it."

"They're out there."

Valerie's eyes took on a thoughtful gleam. "Maybe," she said. Then, rousing herself from some private thought, she said, "Speaking of marriage, have you thought about what you're getting Bliss for a wedding gift?"

"Actually, I have. Do you remember Mittie Powell?"

"The old woman who took you and Bliss in when you were lost in Big Bend?" Valerie asked.

"Yeah."

"She sounded like a character."

"To put it mildly," Logan said dryly. "Well, she called a week or so ago and said that when Bliss spent those few days in Alpine, she'd tried to find out who owned a piece of abandoned property where the two of us took shelter in an old house. Bliss really took a liking to the place. Mittie located the owner, so I made a quick trip to take a look at it and meet with the guy while you two were in Dallas."

"And?" Valerie probed. "How does it look?"

Logan sighed. "There's nothing wrong with the place a small fortune won't fix."

"So it's a money pit," Valerie said with a dismissive wave of her hand. "Are you buying it or not?"

"I've made an offer. I don't know if I'd like to live there full time, but it will make a nice getaway."

Grinning, Russ put a hand over his heart and broke into a husky rendition of "What I Did For Love."

"Laugh if you want, brother. Your day is coming."

"Yeah, right."

"Don't give up, Russell. There's a woman out there somewhere for you," Valerie said, giving him the same pep talk Logan had given her just moments before.

"And speaking of Laura," Logan chimed in, "I made the changes in your will you asked me to."

"What does Laura have to do with finding the right woman for me?" Russ asked his brother.

Logan grinned. "You tell me. You're the one who wanted to change things so she gets a hefty sum if you come to an untimely end."

"That isn't for her," Russ denied. "It's for J.R. I don't want him to do without anything in case I'm not around."

"I thought that's what the trust was for."

Russ felt his face grow hot. "Darn it, Logan!"

"Chill, little brother. It's okay with me if you still feel something for the lady. I like her."

"So do I," Valerie said. "She seems very bright, and she seems to be a good mother."

"She lets that kid get by with murder," Russ said. "What he needs is someone to take him in hand."

"Why don't you apply for the job—full time?"

"Why don't you mind your own business?"

"Boys! Boys! Boys! When are you going to outgrow all this childish squabbling?"

The taunting, sarcastically drawled rebuke came from the dining room doorway. Bliss stood there in her favorite attire of worn jeans and boots, her hair twisted beneath a ball cap with the Campbell Drilling logo emblazoned across the front.

"What are you doing here?" Logan asked getting to his feet and rounding the table.

"I missed you," she said simply, pulling off the cap and sending it sailing across the room toward him. Her hair fell onto her denim-covered shoulders in a sleek, gleaming curtain of natural platinum blond.

Following the hat, she ran across the room, flinging her arms around Logan's neck and jumping up and wrapping her long legs around his waist. They looked at each other for a moment before their mouths met in a hungry kiss.

Russ watched the passion and joy of their reunion, an impassive expression on his face. He stifled a deep sigh. He was happy for his brother, truly happy. But he couldn't deny feeling just a little bit of envy.

Chapter Seven

After tossing and turning until the wee hours, Laura awakened on the Monday following the trip to the Lattimer ranch feeling lethargic, heavy-eyed and more than a little out of sorts.

Exhausted from the intangible but very real tension surrounding her and Russ every time they came within yards of each other, she had expected sleep to come within minutes of her head touching the pillow. Instead, her mind was filled with a jumble of memories—of the time they'd spent together six years before and the times they'd been together since he'd pushed his way into her life and her house a scant week earlier.

The cruel memories answered none of the questions plaguing her. Instead, they taunted her with bittersweet images and impossible dreams of what might have been, if only...

If only Russ, the rich guy with the sexy smile, hard body and devil-may-care attitude hadn't been so attractive.

If only he'd been more responsible.

If only he'd said he loved her.

That's what bothered her the most. She'd known from the beginning that her feelings for him were stronger than his for her, and she'd known that one-sided love affairs always turned out badly. But she hadn't been able to turn off her emotions or stop those feelings from taking root in her heart.

"And here you are," she said out loud, as she poured herself a cup of coffee. "Six years later, raising his son alone, and still feeling things you shouldn't for a man whose sole interest in you is that you bore him a son."

And that, in spades, was the problem. It was why she couldn't sleep, and it was why she was so hateful to Russ whenever he came around. A cantankerous attitude was her only defense against the love she still felt. A love that not only had never died, but one that grew stronger every time they were together, every time she witnessed his earnest expression whenever he spoke to J.R. or saw him smile at their son with that gleam of pride in his eyes.

And every time he looks at you. Or touches you. Don't forget that, Laura.

How could she forget, when she remembered how her pulse started thrumming like a high-powered electric wire whenever he came within a foot of her? How could she forget when the memory of the kiss J.R. had foisted off on them still made her lips tingle like taking a hit from a low-voltage wire, evoking forbidden images of Russ's hard body stroking hers, filling her with a delectable delirium that made her forget upbringing, caution, and precaution.

"Darn it, Laura! Stop mooning around like a six-teen-year-old."

"Who you talking to, Mom?"

She whirled at the sound of J.R.'s voice. He was looking at her with a quizzical expression on his lightly freckled face.

"I was talking to myself, *niño*," she said, thinking that she really had to get herself under control. "What do you want for dinner this evening?"

"Hamburgers," he said without hesitation.

"You got it. Go brush your teeth. I'm running late."

J.R. scampered from the room as the phone rang and she grabbed the cordless from its wall base.

"Hello."

"Hi."

Russ. Her heart sank. Her pulse broke into a sprint. She'd hoped the visit to the ranch would satisfy Russ's newly acquired paternal interest. Obviously, it hadn't. "What do you want?"

His soft laughter sent a frisson of longing down her spine.

"Is that any way to talk to a guy who just made arrangements for you to come to the Saints game next weekend?"

"I beg your pardon?"

"I got tickets for us all to go to the Saints game," he said, his tone pleasant and filled with patience.

"Russ," she said, her equanimity as fragile as parchment, "in case you haven't noticed, I'm a single working mother. I can't afford to fly to New Orleans to watch a football game, even if I wanted to—which

I don't.'' The statement sounded grating, even to her ears.

''I have noticed you're a working mother, and I realize you can't afford to fly over here for what amounts to a whim on my part—said whim being to give my son a chance to watch a live football game because he expressed wanting to do that very much…which is why I arranged for Bliss to fly over and get you.''

She heard him take a deep breath before he plunged ahead.

''And, knowing how you loathe sports, I also realized that you probably didn't want to come to the game, but I figured you wouldn't let J.R. come alone, so I bought you a ticket, anyway.''

One thing about it, when Russ did something, he tried to cover every contingency. ''I can't just drop my life so you can play dad.''

''Then let him come alone. I'll take good care of him.''

''I can't do that, either.''

''Won't, you mean.''

Her light tone was gone. ''All right. Won't.''

''You're smothering him, Laura.''

The accusation sent a sliver of irritation through her. ''What do you mean?''

''You're overprotective.''

Irritation changed to fury. ''Look,'' she said, ''don't go getting any ideas that you know what's best for him after you spent one day together.''

''I know it isn't healthy for him, or any kid who doesn't have to, to stay cooped up inside all day.''

''He has a heart condition, in case you've forgotten.''

"Which can be controlled with medication, in case *you've* forgotten."

Laura compressed her lips. Tears stung her eyes, but they weren't tears of anger. Deep in her heart, she knew Russ was right. J.R. had always spent too much time inside—at least when they were together—even before his heart condition was diagnosed. But there was so much to do when she got in from work that it left precious little time to sit on the back step and watch him play. It was easier to keep him inside where she could keep an eye on him. Still, it cut to the bone to have her efforts criticized, especially by Russ. She'd done her best, darn it.

"He's a boy, Laura," Russ was saying. "He needs to do boy things. He's miserable. Don't turn him into a sissy just because you're worried about him."

Laura latched onto one statement. Her building misery vanished before a new concern. "What do you mean, he's miserable?" she asked in an uncertain tone. "How do you know he is?"

"He told me."

She sank onto one of the kitchen chairs and leaned forward, both elbows on the table. "He told you he was unhappy?"

"Don't put words in my mouth," Russ said, placatingly. "I said he wanted to do something besides play video games. Did you know he loves baseball?"

"I know he watches a lot of it on TV."

"Did you know he wants to be a pitcher when he grows up?"

"No." Her voice sounded small, melancholy, like J.R.'s when he knew he'd done something wrong.

Russ sighed. "Uh-oh. I hear despair in your voice.

Don't beat yourself up over this. You're doing okay. For a single working mom.''

When she didn't come back at him for throwing her words in her face, he said, "You know he wants to play T-ball.''

How had he gotten so much out of Rufio in such a short time? she wondered. More importantly, why had J.R. confided his hopes and dreams to his dad instead of her? She felt a strange combination of pain laced with jealousy, even though the answer was clear. She was too busy trying to keep a roof over their heads to really listen to the child. She wondered again, as she had the day before, if she was sacrificing J.R.'s well-being for her career.

"I knew he wanted to play, but it's impossible.''

"I understand he can't play. Not now, anyway. But there's no reason I can't take him to ball games. And there's no reason I can't buy him a ball and glove and play catch with him, is there? As long as he doesn't overexert himself?''

"Why would you want to do that?'' she asked, rubbing at the frown that had formed between her eyes.

She heard the exasperation in his sigh. "Because he's my son, Laura, and I want him to have what he wants—within reason. I don't want to spoil him, but I do want him to explore his options and to have the opportunity to be a well-rounded person. Don't you think that's important?''

"I suppose, but—''

"It's settled! You're coming over next weekend. Bliss will pick you up Saturday morning. I'll call you later with the time. You can stay at the house.''

Laura felt as if she were being run over by a freight

train. As usual, when Russ got anything that resembled a go-ahead, he did just that—full throttle. She opened her mouth to tell him again that she couldn't go to New Orleans for the weekend, and she certainly couldn't stay with him and his family. The thought of being under the same roof with him for forty-eight hours was more than she could bear. Once again, he seemed to read her mind.

"Don't worry. I won't be there."

She felt a flutter of panic. The thought of *not* having him around was almost as frightening as the idea of being under the same roof with him for a night.

"Logan has some things to talk over with you."

At the mention of Logan, the lawyer, panic and fear raised their menacing heads again. "What kind of things?"

"Nothing to put that scared tone in your voice," he told her, "so calm down. Logan has drawn up some papers for joint custody."

"Joint custody?"

"They're very fair, standard from what Logan says. I'd like to have J.R. every other weekend and a month in the summer. I'll have Logan fax the papers over so your attorney can look at them. If they're okay, he can call in a marker and have a judge sign them while you're here."

"That's big of you," she said, unable to hide her sarcasm.

Russ sighed. "Look, Laura, I don't want to fight with you over this. I don't want to fight with you over anything. I'm only doing this to protect my relationship with my son. If something should happen to you—God forbid—your family might refuse to let me see him. This just keeps things within legal parameters. Okay?''

"Okay," she said grudgingly.

"Good. I'm also going to start sending child support payments every week.''

"Child support?'' She lifted a hand to her whirling head. "I don't want your money!''

"Too bad," he said mildly. "I'm going to give you something for the last five years, too. By the way, when's J.R.'s birthday?''

"April fifth," she said automatically. "Russ, I don't—''

"I've made some changes in my will," he told her, brushing aside any further comments. "And set up a trust for J.R., which is another reason you need to come over. Logan wants to explain some of the details to you just in case I'm not around when J.R. turns twenty-five.''

Laura didn't want to think about that. Her head spun and she felt overwhelmed by the force of his personality...the way she'd always felt around him "Russ. This isn't necessary. I've been doing okay on my own.''

"I don't mean to imply you haven't. From what I see, you've done great, but I don't think you'd deny that having some extra money would eliminate a little strain.''

"You can't buy his love, Russ. And you can't buy your way into my good graces.''

He laughed, but the sound lacked real humor. "Believe me, I know that. Look, I'm not trying to pit what I can give him against what you can. Give me credit for knowing that money isn't love. And I don't want

to take him away from you, Laura, so stop worrying.
I just want to be there for him, too.''

He'd meant what he said, Laura thought as she
drove the few miles to Lillian Hampstead's place on
Thursday morning. If she'd thought—hoped—Russ
would get tired of playing dad, she'd been way off
base. In fact, he called to talk to her or J.R. every
evening.

Though J.R. acted unconcerned when Russ asked
to speak to him, Laura saw how he perked up whenever the phone rang just before his bedtime. Russ
never kept him on the phone long, but the calls were
becoming a habit, and since little hearts could break
so easily, it was a habit she prayed Russ wouldn't
grow tired of. But since he knew plenty about kids
and broken hearts, surely he wouldn't hurt Rufio in-
tentionally.

Laura had had plenty of time to think over what
he'd said about her coddling J.R., too, and while she
suspected she was guilty as charged, she knew it
would be hard to change. Reluctantly, grudgingly, she
acknowledged that just maybe Russ taking part in
J.R.'s life might be a good thing. For J.R., anyway.
How good it would be for her was still debatable.

She'd decided that the only thing she could do was
what she had been doing—keep herself focused on
her job—she had a meeting with the station bigwigs
on Friday—and live her life the way she had been.

One of the things she'd neglected the past couple
of weeks was finishing up the few leads on who had
fathered Russ and Logan. She'd located the two
women whose names Chip Brownlee had given her
and made appointments to meet them the following

week. If they couldn't shed some light on Abby's love life, Chip was lying through his pearly whites or the pregnancy had come about by immaculate conception, Laura thought sardonically. And she wasn't buying the latter. Which is why she was going to see Lillian Hampstead again.

The old woman was vague, at best, and got on Laura's nerves with her infernal rambling about the past—not to mention that she hadn't offered a shred of information that was of any use so far.

She did tell you she remembered a girl giving away one of her twin boys because he had a heart condition.

That was true enough, but that detail hadn't meant a thing until Valerie mentioned Russ's heart problem. Still, Laura felt compelled to tell the former nurse about the mix-up with the two sets of twins. If that didn't jog a cog loose in her age-obstructed memory, nothing would.

"It's worth a shot," Laura mumbled as she pulled into the apartment complex.

Lillian answered the doorbell in a timely manner, a look of surprise on her rouged and powdered face.

"Hello, Mrs. Hampstead. Remember me? Laura Ramirez from the *Dallas Morning News?*"

Lillian cocked her head quizzically. The diamond and ruby studs in her wrinkled earlobes blinked in the October sunshine.

"I'm working on an article about adoptions. And I came to ask you specifically about the Lattimer adoption."

"Oh, yes," Lillian said, the furrow crinkling her forehead smoothing as that bit of memory surfaced. "You said there was something wrong." Thoughtfully, she tapped her bottom lip with a wine-red nail. "What was it, now?"

"There was a twin brother—Zach. Ben Lattimer, who adopted Jake, wondered why the boys were separated."

"Oh, yes!" Lillian said, beaming. "I remember now. I'm afraid you've wasted your time, my dear. I don't remember any more now than I did the first time we talked."

"I appreciate that, Mrs. Hampstead, but I've learned something else that might shed some new light on the subject. Do you mind if I come in?"

Lillian's smile faltered for the briefest time before she said, "Surely, my dear."

She stepped aside for Laura to enter and preceded her into the tasteful, traditional living room. "Please have a seat. I have a pitcher of lovely spiced tea in the refrigerator, if you'd care for a glass."

"Thank you," Laura said with a smile. "That sounds wonderful. Do you need some help?"

Lillian returned the smile and waved away the offer with a blue-veined, beringed hand. "Heavens, no, child. My memory might be fuzzy, but I'm not helpless yet. You just make yourself at home. I'll be right back."

She crossed the room, turning at the doorway. "Would you like some fresh mint? I grow it in my windowsill."

"Yes, thank you," Laura said, taking a seat at one end of the elegant camel-back sofa.

As Lillian disappeared into the kitchen, Laura chided herself for her uncharitable thoughts. The old woman was really charming...in a peculiar sort of way. But there was something Laura couldn't quite put her finger on—an occasional calculating look in her eyes, an infrequent and unexpected rigidity in her manner—that gave the impression the woman might be charming in her dotage but had been hell on wheels in her prime.

"Here we are," Lillian said, her entrance into the room scattering Laura's thoughts.

She set the silver tray on the coffee table and handed Laura a frosty glass and a cloth napkin. While Lillian settled into a chair across the table, Laura took a drink of the tea, letting the flavors of orange and cinnamon tantalize her taste buds. "This is delicious," she said, meaning every word.

"Thank you. It's my mother's recipe." She frowned and said, "Or was it Aunt Catherine's?" The look she gave Laura was both apologetic and whimsical. "I really can't remember. But I don't suppose it matters as long as it's tasty, does it?"

Lillian took a small sip and leaned back in her chair. "What was it you came to see me about?"

"The Lattimer adoption thirty-five years ago," Laura reminded her gently. "The fact that one of your patients had twins, and Ben and Retha Lattimer adopted one of them."

Lillian's lips pursed thoughtfully. "Oh, yes." Her eyes twinkled with a naughty gleam. "As I recall, Ben Lattimer was a right handsome man."

Laura smiled. "He still is. Do you remember that Ben found out the child he adopted had an identical twin?"

"He did?" Lillian said as if it were the first time she'd heard the news. "Then why didn't he adopt them both?"

Laura stifled a sigh of frustration. What hope she'd

had that Lillian might remember something—anything—to help her was rapidly disappearing.

"The last time I was here, you told me you remembered one of your patients having twins. She
was supposed to adopt them out, but in the end she
couldn't bring herself to. You said she kept one but
gave up the other because it had a heart condition."

"Oh, yes!" Lillian smiled. "I do remember. A little blond girl. Sweet as can be. A preacher's daughter,
I think."

"That's right!"

Zach had told Laura his maternal grandfather was
a preacher. The fact that Lillian recalled this much
about Abby boded well. Maybe this trip would pro-
duce something new, after all.

"Her name was Abby Pickett, and yes, she was a
preacher's daughter. The problem is that Jake Lattimer, the child she gave up because he had a heart
condition, doesn't have one."

"I don't imagine her daddy was too happy about
the whole thing," Lillian said, ignoring Laura's statement. "Him being a man of God and all."

"I'm sure it was hard on everyone," Laura agreed,
wondering how she could bring Lillian's wandering
mind to the problem. "Ms. Hampstead, do you remember Jack and Valerie Campbell?"

"Like the soup?"

"Yes, like the soup."

"No." She squinted thoughtfully at Laura. "Oh,
dear. I have a feeling I should remember, shouldn't
I?" She lowered her shamed eyes to the napkin-
wrapped glass she held clutched in her lap.

Laura nodded. "She and her husband were on their

way to Houston when she went into labor. She was at the hospital the same night Abby Pickett was.''

Lillian lifted a troubled countenance to Laura. "It was a terrible night, you know. Storming. We didn't have any phones, and the doctor couldn't get there. We were run ragged, I remember that.''

"Yes, you told me," Laura said patiently.

Lillian looked embarrassed. "That's right, I did.''

"Do you remember Valerie Campbell giving birth to twins, too.''

"Twins? No.'' She smiled, a soft, dreamlike smile. "Twins," she said again. "How lovely.''

Laura sighed in frustration. "Ms. Hampstead, there's a problem.''

"Oh, dear!" Lillian said, rising. "Is something wrong with the tea?''

"No! Please sit down. The tea is fine. Delicious, in fact.''

Clearly confused, Lillian lowered herself into the chair. "Then what's the problem?''

"The problem is that you said Abby gave away the baby with the heart problem, but he's never had one. Neither has his brother, Zach. When I spoke with Valerie Campbell recently, she told me her son, Russ, had suffered from a heart problem as a child, but he outgrew it.''

"That's wonderful, then, isn't it?''

"It is, certainly, but don't you see what I'm getting at?''

"I'm sorry, dear. I'm afraid I don't.''

"They were switched," Laura told her.

"Switched?" Lillian's carefully arched eyebrows drew together. "Who was switched?''

"The two sets of twins. Valerie and Jack Campbell's boys were somehow mixed up with Abby Pickett's sons.''

Lillian's face grew red. Laura thought she saw a hint of anger in the faded blue eyes.

"Oh, no," the old nurse said, setting down her glass with a thud. "That's impossible. My nurses were the best."

Laura set her glass on the coffee table and leaned forward earnestly. "I don't mean to imply that someone didn't do their job properly, Mrs. Hampstead. I'm just suggesting…"

She paused, took another tack. "It seems to me Russ Campbell's heart condition proves that someone inadvertently switched Abby Pickett's babies with the Campbell children. It could have happened easily if there was as much confusion as everyone claims."

The color in Lillian's face receded as Laura spoke. There was a suspicion of tears in her eyes. "You're right. Of course it could have happened, but it's just hard for me to believe…I was the charge nurse. I should have noticed something was wrong."

"Don't blame yourself," Laura consoled her. "It's just one of those freak things. It could have happened to anyone. The important thing is that the truth was found out. Or most of the truth, anyway," she added.

Lillian raised a teary gaze to Laura's. "Oh, dear. Don't tell me there are other problems."

"Not a problem, really. But since we know now that Jake Lattimer and Zach Rawlings are actually Jack and Valerie Campbell's birth sons, we're in the dark about who fathered Logan and Russ Campbell, who were born to Abby Pickett."

"It is a tangle, isn't it?" Lillian said, a troubled expression in her eyes.

"Did she say anything to you, Ms. Hampstead?"

Lillian frowned, obviously not following. "Who, dear?"

"Abby Pickett. I know her parents placed her in your home during her pregnancy. Since she was there several months, I thought maybe you got to know her and she confided in you."

Lillian straightened her already straight spine.

"I wasn't there to be their friend, Miss Ramirez. I was there to guide them through a difficult time."

"But surely befriending them was part of that. They were young and lonely. They must have needed someone to talk to."

"I ran the business end of things. If they talked to anyone, it would have been Ruthie."

"Ruthie?" A thought, almost a moment of recognition, flitted through Laura's mind, but before she could latch onto it, it was gone, leaving her with the distinct feeling she was missing something.

"Ruthie." A look of embarrassment passed over Lillian's face. "Oh, dear, I can't remember her last name, but she cooked and cleaned and played mother to the girls."

"Do you know how I can get in touch with her?"

"Oh, my, no! I haven't seen her in years. I'd have no idea where to find her. I believe she had a sister who lived in the Dallas area, though, if that's any help."

Oh, yeah. That was tons of help. It would be real easy to find Ruthie with no last name through a sister who didn't have a name in a place the size of Dallas. Laura breathed out a slow hiss of disappointment. Every time a door opened and she thought she was close to finding out something, the door slammed in her face.

She forced a smile. "What about your personal records? Do you think you might have an old address or the name of an emergency contact person for Ruthie? Her sister, maybe?"

"All the home's records are in storage."

Laura chewed on her bottom lip. "Wouldn't Abby have had to put the father's name on the birth certificate?"

"Not necessarily. She could have put father unknown. But even if she did name him, it was a closed adoption, and the records are sealed."

Another slammed door. Laura sighed. "That's that, then," she said standing. "I won't take any more of your time."

"I can see you're disappointed," Lillian Hampstead said, getting to her feet. "I'm sorry my memory is so fuzzy."

"On the contrary," Laura said gallantly. "You've been a great help, Mrs. Hampstead. Thank you."

"You're quite welcome. I'll see you out."

"Don't bother. I know the way." Thanking the old woman again, Laura crossed the living room and let herself out, rummaging for her car keys as she made her way to her car.

What now? She unlocked the door of her car. Where could she go from here? She was running out of leads—and fast. She hated coming up empty-handed, especially since Logan wanted so badly to find out who his father was.

She, too, was curious about the man who'd fathered Logan and Russ. Partly because she hated unsolved riddles, and partly because she was naturally curious about the man whose genes had contributed to Russ and Rufio's character. She hoped that whoever he was, he was a man like Ben Lattimer. Honorable, honest and caring. If he was a Chip Brownlee type... Laura shuddered delicately and started the car.

Besides Abby's two classmates, who else could she talk to? What loose thread had she neglected to pull? She was almost home when it occurred to her that Tom Barnette might remember the name of the woman who'd worked for Lillian. With a full name to work with, there was no telling what Laura might find out.

Not only that, but Tom should be informed that twins had been separated that night, and had been switched—not that telling him would solve anything. He'd claimed innocence to the knowledge that Jake Lattimer was born a twin, and even though Laura didn't like Barnette—as a man or a politician—something told her he was telling the truth...at least about that.

She scrolled through the battery-operated organizer she kept in the car and located Barnette's number, which she punched into the cell phone.

"Barnette and Sandifer." The voice was middle-aged and pleasant. "This is Cora. How may I help you?"

"Hi, Cora. This is Laura Ramirez with the *Dallas Morning News*. I was in a few weeks ago to talk with Mr. Barnette about an article I was working on. I wonder if I could have a few minutes with him. I have a couple of quick questions."

"Of course I remember. I'm sorry, Ms. Ramirez, but Mr. Barnette is leaving for an appointment within the hour. He's trying to clear his desk."

The friendliness in the woman's voice had been replaced with a wary determination. With the Aegean Insurance mess hanging over his perfectly styled, graying head, no doubt old Tom had instructed his receptionist to keep any and all news hounds at bay.

Disappointment and relief vied for control of Laura's emotions. The last thing she wanted to do was spend any considerable time chatting with Barnette. On the other hand, if he could give her Ruthie's last name, she might be able to track down the name of the man Abby Pickett had been so secretive about.

"Look, Cora," she said patiently. "I'm not calling to grill him about Aegean Insurance. I have some information to pass on to him about something that happened thirty-five years ago at the Brownsboro home for unwed mothers. I'd like to ask him if he remembers an employee who worked there."

There was a lengthy pause while Cora weighed what she'd heard. Then she said, "Just a moment, please."

In a matter of seconds, Tom Barnette came on the line. "You have two minutes, Ms. Ramirez. I'm a busy man."

Laura held the receiver at arm's length and blinked at it in surprise. The ultra-smooth, unruffled man she'd spoken to had disappeared. This Tom Barnette sounded harried, pressured...ready to snap.

"I'm calling to see if you remember the name of the woman who did the cooking and cleaning at the home. Lillian said it was Ruthie someone, but she couldn't remember the last name."

"Why on earth would you need to talk to the housekeeper?" Barnette asked.

"Mrs. Hampstead thought this Ruthie person might be able to answer some questions for me."

"Do you mind telling me why you're intent on pursuing this?"

"It isn't me, Mr. Barnette. I'm following up on this at the request of Zach Rawlings and Jake Lattimer."

"I'm sorry, Ms. Ramirez, but I don't have time for this nonsense. Now if you'll excuse me, I have an appointment."

Before Laura could reply, she heard the sound of buzzing in her ear.

Tom Barnette had hung up on her.

Chapter Eight

"Back to square one," she murmured, ending the connection on her cell phone. She pulled into her regular parking place at the *News* office.

She'd go visit the two women Chip had told her about, and if they couldn't tell her anything about Abby's past, she'd have to tell Logan she'd done all she could. He and Russ would have to learn to live with the idea that they might never know who their real father was.

In the meantime, she wanted to clear her desk before she took off for her New Orleans weekend, and she needed to do some polishing on her article. The first of its six parts was due to run in Sunday's paper. It was imperative that the article be her best effort, since the boys in power at the television station were watching everything she did with more than a little interest.

She grabbed her briefcase from the seat and slammed the car door. Every time she thought of how Russ had finagled her into agreeing to spend the weekend with him, she felt like screaming. He might say that the time they'd be spending together was to build a relationship with Rufio, and that was true, but it was also true that she'd be spending time with them both, and she wasn't sure she wanted to spend two days watching her son grow more attached to his father.

Get real, Laura. What you're really afraid of is that you'll become more attached to him, too.

With her heart beating double time and her stomach quivering with nerves, Laura drove herself and J.R. to Love Field early the following Saturday morning. Russ wanted them to fly over early so they could have more of the day to play.

Bliss might have gotten older, but physically, she hadn't changed much since the Odessa blowout. The leggy blonde in the royal blue flight suit was easy to spot, even though it was barely daylight. She stood next to a brand-new white twin-engine six-seater with a scarlet B and A superimposed over a royal blue B and A. Big Easy Charters was painted beneath.

"Where's the plane?" J.R. asked, pressing his nose to the window.

"The white and blue one over there," Laura said, pointing as she maneuvered the car into a parking place. "See the lady in blue? That's Bliss."

"Wow!" J.R. said in an awe-filled voice. "Are we going to go up in *that?*"

"'Fraid so," Laura said, dreading the thought.

"Cool," J.R. said in a voice bordering on reverence.

Cool, my foot! Laura thought. She was a poor flyer at best, and small planes terrified her. She didn't relish the idea of going up in a plane so small God could flick it out of the sky with one negligent swish of His pinkie.

Laura unbuckled J.R.'s seat belt. He got out of the car and went around to the trunk as she instructed. She was trying her best to teach him responsibility by letting him help whenever possible.

She was unlocking the trunk when a slightly familiar feminine voice said, "Need some help?"

Laura turned and saw Bliss coming toward them with an easy loose-gaited stride, her platinum hair blowing in the October breeze.

"Hello, Bliss," she said when the other woman came to a stop a few feet away. "And thanks. You're looking particularly wonderful."

A sultry, satisfied smile spread over Bliss's features. "Love of a good man," she said in a voice that matched her expression. Her sapphire-hued gaze raked Laura from head to toe. "You haven't exactly gone into a decline yourself."

"Thanks," Laura said. "You made my day."

The compliment, coming from another woman, was a boost to her self-esteem. With her hectic work schedule, worry about landing the new job and trying to see to it that she spent quality time with Rufio, there was seldom any time left over for herself. She was doing good to make sure body, hair and teeth were clean before she fell into bed, too exhausted most nights to even dream. She hadn't put any polish on her nails in months, hadn't conditioned her hair in weeks, hadn't exercised in days. She'd been feeling fragmented, frazzled and frowzy...more so since Russ had charged back into her life.

"New plane?" Laura asked, reaching for the first bag.

Bliss's countenance brightened considerably. "Yeah. I've gone into the charter business with a buddy—Buzz Anderson."

"Russ mentioned you were thinking about it."

"Do you like the logo? We couldn't come up with anything really sharp, so we doubled up on our initials. You know Bliss Abernathy...Buzz Anderson?"

"It catches the eye," Laura said, nodding.

"Great." Bliss smiled and squatted to Rufio's level. "Hi. You must be J.R.," she said, offering him her hand. "I've heard a lot about you."

"I'll bet," Laura said with a lift of her eyebrows. Bliss laughed.

Fortunately, the byplay went over J.R.'s head. "Hi," he said, taking Bliss's hand. "You must be my almost aunt Bliss."

The smile on Bliss's face widened. "That I am. But you can go ahead and call me Aunt Bliss now. Do you like to fly?"

"I don't know," J.R. said solemnly. "I've never done it before." Neither Laura nor Bliss could miss the excitement shimmering in the depths of his eyes.

"Well, then, it's about time you did, don't you think?"

"Yes ma'am."

"Let's get your gear loaded, and we'll take off."

Laura watched with a combination of amazement and amusement as J.R. grabbed her overnight bag with both hands and lugged it toward the waiting aircraft.

"You certainly lit a fire under him. I have to beg him to do anything for me."

Bliss grinned. "I just pushed the right button. Speaking of which, what have you done to Russ?"

Laura hefted J.R.'s duffel bag out of the trunk. "What do you mean?" she asked with a frown.

"I mean that my best friend has been a mess ever since he found out about J.R."

"A mess?"

"Yeah. He's always had enough energy for three people, but he's been bouncing off the walls the past couple of weeks. He's driving everyone crazy about this weekend. He's changed the menu so often that Sophie is about ready to coldcock him with a rolling pin. He's imagined putting you in every guest room in the house."

"Any place is fine," Laura said, unsettled at the thought of their visit causing such a stir.

"When he complained about the morning light in the last room Valerie suggested, and she told him she felt sure that if it suited the governor and his wife it would suit you, I think he realized what an ass he was being."

Hot color stained Laura's cheeks. What on earth did she think she was doing trying to fit in with people who hobnobbed with the governor of Louisiana, for goodness sake!

"We shouldn't have come," she said. "I don't want to be any trouble for anyone."

"It isn't you. It's Russ," Bliss said with a grin. "He's made so many changes in his will and drawn up so many papers about this and that, he's about to drive Logan nuts." She paused. "Oops. Maybe I shouldn't have said anything."

"It's all right," Laura said. "He told me. As a matter of fact, I'm supposed to meet with Logan while I'm here to go over some things."

"That's great, then," Bliss said, relief glowing in her eyes. She cocked her head toward J.R. "One thing for sure, that little guy's financial future is mapped out."

Laura knew the statement was meant to reassure her, instead she felt the anger that simmered just below the surface of her emotions begin to roil.

"I told Russ that J.R. and I don't need his money!" she said. "I don't want it. And J.R. can darn well work for whatever he wants for his future, the way most of the rest of the world has to do."

Shock left Bliss speechless. She stared into Laura's angry eyes for long seconds. Finally, she said, "I think Russ just wants to make sure that whatever J.R. wants to do is made a little easier by having a strong financial backing. You know as well as I do that it's a lot easier to perform up to par when you aren't worried about how to pay the electric bill."

The quiet censure in Bliss's voice sent a wave of remorse through Laura. She felt like an ungrateful clod, which, of course, she was. "I'm sorry. It's just that I've done okay without him and his money, and no matter what he gives me or J.R., it can't make up for his not being around the past six years."

"I know that, and so does Russ, but it won't keep him from trying."

What Bliss said was true. Russ might have been a little wild and a lot irresponsible in the past, but he was generous to a fault, and there wasn't a truly mean bone in his body.

J.R. ran up, exasperation on his face. "Come on, Mom. Let's go!"

"I'm sorry, Rufio," she said, forcing a smile for his benefit. "Bliss and I were talking." She handed him the strap of a floral tapestry Pullman. "See if you can get that over to the plane."

J.R. hoisted the strap over his shoulder and took off across the tarmac, dragging the suitcase slowly behind him. Laura reached in for a mesh bag filled with toys—just in case he got bored with whatever plans Russ had cooked up for the weekend. Bliss picked up J.R.'s duffel bag, and Laura slammed the trunk shut.

"Car locked?" Bliss asked.

Laura nodded, and they started toward the plane.

Bliss stowed the luggage and helped them get settled. To both J.R. and Laura's pleasure, Bliss put the child in the seat beside her, so she could explain the workings of the instruments to him and, she said, riffling his hair, so he could have a bird's-eye view. The arrangement suited Laura just fine, thank you very much. She got vertigo standing on a kitchen stool.

Confident—or as confident as she could be considering her considerable fear of flying—that they were in good hands with Bliss as the pilot, Laura leaned her head against the seat and closed her eyes. The sounds of Bliss and J.R.'s voices blended with the hum of the engines, lulling her to a semiconscious state where her mind drifted and wandered along the edges of wakefulness. Once the plane took a severe dip, sending Laura's eyelids flying upward and her heart and stomach diving before it leveled out once more.

"Watch the instrument panel, J.R. You've gotta keep the horizon straight," Bliss said patiently, "or we'll wind up a greasy spot somewhere."

Rufio laughed, but the laughter sounded shaky. "Maybe you'd better do it."

Good grief, Laura thought, Bliss had actually let him fly the plane, though Laura noticed that her hands were curled confidently on the other set of controls. Relieved that for once J.R. seemed to realize his limitations, Laura closed her eyes again.

In what seemed like a very short time, he was announcing—per Bliss's instructions—that they were making their final approach to the runway and for all passengers to please fasten their seat belts. Laura heard him but was too relaxed to move. Or maybe she just wanted to keep her eyes closed and try to forget that she'd soon be facing Russ and the entire Campbell clan on their turf.

"Mom!" J.R. cried, "wake up! We're almost there."

"I'm awake!" she said, pushing herself upright. She turned from the window so she wouldn't see the ground rushing up to meet them and held her breath as Bliss brought the small aircraft to a stop. Only then did she release her death grip on the armrests and draw in a normal breath of air.

Adopting a prim, monotone voice, Bliss said, "We've reached our destination, and thank you again for flying Big Easy Charters." Grinning, she turned to J.R. "Okay, big guy, you can undo your seat belt now."

J.R. was out of his seat in a flash, flinging himself

into Laura's arms, a wide, happy smile on his face. "I flew the plane, Mom. All by myself."

"You did?" she asked. "All by yourself?"

"Well," he amended, "Aunt Bliss had her hands on the controls, too, just in case."

Laura held him close and pressed a kiss to his bright curls. "Did you thank Aunt Bliss for letting you sit up front and explaining how the plane works?"

He pulled back to look at her and shook his head. "I should, huh?"

"I think that would be nice."

He tore free of her embrace and made his way toward Bliss, who was going through her usual on-ground ritual. Halfway there, he turned and asked, "Mom, do you think Bobby Preston has ever flown a plane before?"

"I doubt it," she replied. "I'll bet his aunt doesn't own her own plane, either."

"Way cool," J.R. said, doing his utmost to suppress a pleased grin...and failing.

Laura watched with surprise as he put his arms around Bliss's neck and murmured, "Thanks, Aunt Bliss."

Bliss met Laura's gaze over J.R.'s head. The expression on her face was something between disbelief and wonder.

A banging at the door sent J.R. whirling around.

"That's probably your dad," Bliss said.

J.R.'s face fell. He was excited about the trip and all the things he was going to get to do, but he still wasn't sure how he felt about Russ.

"He's been anxious for you to get here," Bliss told him, seeing the look on J.R.'s face and knowing he and Russ hadn't gotten off to the best of starts. "He's got a lot of neat stuff planned for you to do." When J.R. didn't reply, she said, "Come on. I'll show you how to open the hatch."

As soon as the door swung aside and the steps were lowered, Russ poked his head in, finding Laura's gaze with the unerring accuracy of a compass needle finding north. Her heart took the same breath-stealing dip it had when J.R. let the nose of the plane drop.

Russ was gorgeous, as usual, she thought with something akin to dismay. The gold and brown plaid of his shirt went nicely with his coloring. The hint of beard—he obviously hadn't taken time to shave yet—gave him an exciting, dangerous look.

She resisted the vanity-inspired impulse to smooth her hair, which she'd caught up in a saucy ponytail for the trip. Why hadn't she taken the time to put on her makeup, even though she'd had to get up at the crack of dawn? When was the last time she'd had a facial? And did the pasty whiteness her face had no doubt taken on during the flight go with the bright yellow of her blouse?

"Hi, big brother," Bliss said, stepping between them and reaching out so Russ could help her out of the plane. "Long time no see."

"At least eight hours," he drawled, swinging her down. "How's the plane?"

"Handles like a dream. Buzz told me she was nice, but she's *really* nice."

"That's great. If you'll open the hold, I'll help carry the bags to the truck."

"Roger." Bliss disappeared, and Russ once again focused his attention on the plane's two passengers.

"Hi." To Laura's relief, the salutation was directed at J.R.

"Hi." The enthusiasm J.R. had shown so far on the trip had been secluded somewhere in his psyche.

"How was the trip?" The question was spoken to J.R., but Russ's gaze rested on Laura.

"Fine."

"He took the controls for a minute or so," Bliss called.

"No kidding?" Russ asked, his eyebrows raised in disbelief.

J.R. nodded.

"Do you think Bobby Preston has ever held the controls of a plane? Even for a minute or so?" Russ asked.

Rufio shook his head. "I doubt it."

"Me, too." Russ reached out his arms. "Come on. Let's help Aunt Bliss get the luggage."

J.R. hesitated, then let his dad lift him down.

Russ stepped up a step. His bulky shoulders filled the small hatch. There was nothing between him and Laura but the width of the plane's interior, which wasn't nearly enough, she thought on a wave of panic.

"You look like hell."

Her surprise came out in a burst of breathless, self-deprecating laughter. "Thank you very much."

Russ swore. "I'm sorry. That didn't come out the way I meant it to. I just meant you look a little off color. I'd forgotten you hate to fly."

"Apology accepted," she said, turning away from the intensity in his eyes and gathering her purse. She crossed the narrow cabin and paused in the opening of the hatch. "Excuse me."

Instead of moving, Russ reached out for her, the way he had for Bliss and J.R.

She didn't want to touch him, to feel the warmth and hardness of his body through his shirt. She didn't want to feel his hands on her waist or experience the power of his arms. Doing so would only bring another rush of those wonderful, dreaded memories of his hands moving over her body, and his strength and stamina as they'd made love far into the night.

Unfortunately, she didn't have an option. He had no intention of moving. Releasing a resigned sigh, she slipped the strap of her purse over her shoulder and reached out to brace her hands on his shoulders. She felt his hands span her waist.

For the briefest of moments, neither moved as the warmth of memories swirled around them, washing over them like the slow ebb and flow of the tide at the end of a sultry summer day. It was crazy to feel this, to feel anything for him. Not only crazy, but dangerous, especially since she'd been working over-time to convince herself that what they'd once felt for each other was as cold as the Odessa well fire.

His hands held her securely, and even though his touch was impersonal, she felt it to the center of her soul. She'd been right. He was warm...and strong. Her hands itched to delve beneath the cotton pullover and reacquaint themselves with the way that warmth and strength combined with strong bone and fluid muscle.

The scent of him drifted to her, filling her nostrils with the clean, green scent of some expensive soap. It would taste bitter, like perfume, against her tongue, she thought, letting her gaze climb from the placket of his shirt to his eyes. And his skin would be salty and smooth....

His smile was lazy, almost teasing. "We've got us a bona fide problem here."

The comment, delivered in a husky rumble that seemed to emanate from his very soul, brought Laura to her senses with painful abruptness. She tried to pull free, but he held her tightly.

"There's no problem."

"You're right," he said. "Nothing that a quick trip to the hot tub wouldn't cure."

Laura sucked in a shocked breath. The memory, one of her most dreaded and tantalizing favorites, hung between them, filling their minds with thoughts and images that had no place in their wary cease-fire.

"Let go, Russ," she said, her voice a breathless whisper. At that moment, she wanted nothing more than to put as much distance as possible between them.

"God knows I've tried," he said, an earnest, almost angry look in his eyes, "and I thought I had, but lately I'm not so sure."

The confession was as much a shock to her as the forbidden feelings that besieged them moments before. It took their relationship—if that's what it was—in a new and totally unexpected direction.

Not really.

If she were honest, she'd admit that a part of her had hoped he would feel those feelings for her again. On the other hand, if he did, and she acted on them, she'd open up herself—and J.R.—for more heartbreak.

"This is ridiculous." She spoke the words in a low, fierce voice.

"I agree. But it's there, isn't it?"
"No!"
"Liar."

They were having lunch in the conservatory, since, as Valerie put it, her orchids were putting on a show. The morning had been spent visiting and touring the huge house, complete with library and billiard room.

J.R., in typical fashion—or with a kid's knack for cutting to the chase—had summed it up. "Wow! Grandma Valerie lives in the Clue house." Everyone had laughed, but Laura fully expected Colonel Mustard or Miss Peacock to show up at any second.

The Gaspard mansion was all and more than she expected, certainly not a setting she'd ever feel comfortable in. She hadn't felt so much like a fish out of water since the days of her whirlwind affair with Russ. Even J.R. had been impressed as Russ led them to their room. She only hoped that awe would keep him on his best behavior.

She realized her feelings of insecurity had everything to do with her attitude. She'd been shown nothing but warmth ever since she and J.R. had been ushered into the marble foyer.

Now, as she entered the conservatory, lush with green and growing things whose names she'd never heard of, she felt that self-doubt creeping back in. She watched Russ move the centerpiece of fresh-cut roses a fraction of an inch. The butler, Dalton, shook his head, a look of patience molding his sharp features.

"Wow!" J.R. said, as Laura led him through the French doors, "Grandma Val has a garden inside her house."

"It's called a conservatory," Laura told him. "And

don't pick any flowers," she added in a harsh whisper.

"I call it a greenhouse," Russ said, strolling toward them, his hands plunged into the pockets of his chocolate-hued slacks.

"Where is everyone?" Laura asked, needing the buffer of more people.

"Logan and Bliss will be down in a few minutes. Mom, too. She got a call from Ben as she started down."

"Oh."

With unintentional gesture of mimicry, Laura plunged her hands into the pockets of the green and blue tartan jacket she wore over a forest green sheath dress and searched her mind for something intelligent to say.

Russ smiled at J.R. "How do you like your room?"

"It's big."

Russ nodded and turned to Laura. "And yours?"

"It's fine." Seeing the look on his face, she recanted. "I don't mean *just* fine. It's better than fine. It's wonderful. I love white on white, but I'm afraid to have anything too light with a usually grubby little boy running in and out."

Russ's smile stopped her heart. "I can see how that could be a problem."

"Do you live here?" J.R. asked. Laura had been curious about that herself, but would never have had the courage to ask.

"No," Russ replied. "I usually live in a forty-foot travel trailer wherever we're drilling for oil."

"Like a mobile home?" J.R. asked.

"Exactly. Unless there's some reason for me to

stay here overnight, I stay in the trailer when we're between jobs.''

"Did you and my mom get a divorce?"

"J.R.!" Laura cried, aghast. Where on earth had that come from?

"It's okay," Russ said. "No, we aren't divorced. We were never married."

"Why not?"

"I beg your pardon," Russ said, taken aback by J.R.'s persistence.

"Most moms and dads are married. If they aren't married, then they got a divorce.''

Laura was torn between embarrassment and a quietly breaking heart. Poor little guy! He was doing his best to put together the pieces in some way he could understand.

"Well, your mom and I aren't married because she never asked me.''

Laura's shocked gaze flew to his.

"Why?" J.R. asked again.

"Probably because I wasn't very nice back when we knew each other before you were born."

"Did you yell at her a lot back then, too?"

It was Russ's turn to be disconcerted. Though she was appalled by Rufio's questions, it gave Laura a perverse sense of pleasure to see a dull crimson creep into Russ's cheeks.

Glancing at her, he surprised the look of satisfaction in her eyes. His gaze meshed with hers. He said, "No, I didn't yell at her at all back then. I kissed her."

Laura's mouth dropped open in an O of surprise.

"I kissed her a lot."

"Why do you yell at her now? Like that day you first came to our house?"

"Because I was mad at her for doing something I didn't think she should have done." The answer was for J.R., but he spoke to Laura. "I was wrong. She was doing her job, and just because it made me unhappy, she did the right thing."

Laura looked into the sincerity of his amber eyes and knew it was as close as an apology as she was likely to get for uncovering—however innocently—the truth about his past.

Russ turned his attention to J.R. "If she hadn't been doing her job, and if I'd never gotten mad at her, I would never have come to Dallas to tell her off, and I might never have found out about you, and that would have made me very sad."

"It would?" J.R. asked. "Even if I squirted catsup on Leza and fell in the pool and scared you?"

Russ nodded. "Even if."

J.R. thought about that for a moment. Laura heard Bliss and Logan's voices drawing nearer.

"Sorry we're late," Bliss said, her breezy entrance silencing J.R. "We had some important things to take care of."

"Yeah, I'll just bet you did," Russ said.

Thankfully, the innuendo went over J.R.'s head.

"We had to take care of some *wedding plans*," Bliss said, stressing the words. "Honeymoon plans, to be exact. We had to make a final decision about whether to go to Greece or Rome and make some arrangements about renting a villa, you dirty old man."

Russ held up his hands, palms outward. "My apologies.'' He glanced at the utilitarian Timex strapped to his wrist. "I'm starving. What's keeping Mom?''

"I'm here!'' Valerie said, almost running into the room. Her color was high, and her eyes gleamed. "I'm sorry to hold things up.''

"No problem,'' Logan told her. "Bliss and I just came down.''

"What did Ben want?'' Russ asked.

Laura thought Valerie's color deepened. "He's coming over for a meeting next week and wondered if we could get together for lunch while he was in town.''

Russ and Logan exchanged amused glances. Valerie didn't miss the byplay.

"Oh, come on, you two. It isn't as if it's a date or anything. It's just a couple of old friends getting together for lunch.''

"You don't have to defend your actions to us,'' Russ said.

"Then why do I feel like I do?''

"Guilty conscience?''

"Russell!''

He laughed and flung an arm around her shoulders. "Just teasing, Mom. You take it so poorly.''

"Then why do you do it?''

"Because it's fun.''

Valerie cast Laura an exasperated look. "Now you know where J.R. gets it.''

"What if Ben wanted to get serious?'' Bliss asked.

"He doesn't,'' Valerie insisted. "But if he did, let's just say that he's one of the few men I'd consider getting serious with.'' She looked from Bliss to one son and then other. "Now, if everyone's curiosity about the state of my love life—or lack of it—has been satisfied, I'll have Dalton serve lunch.''

Russ threw up his hands. "I'm cool."

"Me, too," Logan and Bliss echoed.

"Laura, I apologize."

"Not necessary," she said, smiling at her hostess. She'd enjoyed the easy camaraderie she felt among the Campbells, just as she'd liked hearing about where Russ lived when he wasn't at the Gaspard mansion.

Strangely, none of the group seemed corrupted by their considerable wealth. Maybe, she thought, that had been Jack Campbell's contribution to his family. A firm grasp of reality, a solid grip on the things that really mattered.

Valerie smiled and nodded to Dalton, who moved silently from the room. Then she held out her hand to J.R., who took it without a second's hesitation.

"To quote your dad, I'm starving. Let's eat."

When they were all seated, J.R. turned to Russ. "Why didn't you ask her?"

"Ask who what?" Russ queried, failing to make J.R.'s mental leap of logic.

"If Mom didn't ask you to marry her, why didn't you ask her?"

"J.R.!" she said, once again stunned by his audacity and the fact that he'd asked the question in front of the whole family. Every eye seemed to move from J.R. to her. She knew they were all wondering what they'd missed before.

"It's okay, J.R.," Russ said. His gaze panned the

group. "J.R. wanted to know why Laura and I aren't married. Earlier I told him it was because she didn't ask me."

He met the query in J.R.'s eyes without flinching. "I didn't ask *her*," he said, "because I was a fool."

Chapter Nine

On Sunday morning, Laura showered and dressed for the football game that afternoon. Logan had left early for the Gaspard Building to take care of a minor legal emergency. She and Russ were to meet him there at nine-thirty, while Bliss and Valerie kept J.R. entertained. After they finished discussing J.R.'s future, she, Russ and Logan were going to buy a copy of the *Dallas Morning News* so she could see the first instalment of "Adoption—Then and Now." Then they would rendezvous at the Café du Monde for a late breakfast with the rest of the family before caravaning to the Superdome.

Laura wasn't looking forward to being alone with Russ, even for the length of time it took to drive from the Garden District to the Gaspard offices. His declaration the day before of not asking her to marry him because he'd been a fool had left her feeling strangely unsettled.

The statement had been more than a confession that he'd made a mistake. It had been an admission that he'd cared for her more than he wanted to admit...maybe more than he'd realized. She'd thought she had her feelings for him pigeonholed, but hearing his reply and sensing his vulnerability made her realize that maybe he had changed, that maybe he had regrets about the past, too.

So where does that leave you, Laura?

Exactly where she had been, she told herself, even though she knew that wasn't true. Hearing him say he'd been a fool not to marry her satisfied the part of her that was wholly and innately woman. The simple statement, spoken quietly in front of his whole family, had lain heavy on her soul, finding that one spot in her heart that hadn't completely hardened against him and working some arcane bit of magic that was subtly altering her feelings for him.

Though she refused to give free rein to those feelings, at strange times during the remainder of the previous day, she'd found herself thinking that there might be a chance....

A chance for what? A rosy, happily-ever-after life together? Come on, Laura, you haven't believed in fairy tales for a long time.

Maybe that was the problem. Maybe she'd been too busy dealing with reality the past few years to believe in things like fantasies and miracles. Yet wasn't the serendipitous reunion of Zach and Jake and the subsequent uncovering of the truth about what had happened to them something of a miracle—especially the

way it had all worked to bring Russ back into her
life?

Just when you needed him the most.

The thought stilled the brush she dragged through
her dark hair with long, rhythmic strokes. It was time
to put aside her mixed emotions about him and give
him the benefit of the doubt, take his interest in J.R.
at face value and at least consider whatever arrangements he had in mind for their son's future with im-
partiality. After all, no matter what feelings there still
might be between them, the more she watched him
and J.R. together, the more convinced she was that
his interest in his son was genuine and not just a
passing fancy.

"How long will this take?" Laura asked as they
stepped into the Gaspard Building's ancient elevator.
After spending the drive over in a silence that raised
her general level of discomfort, her nerves were
stretched to the limit.

"Not long," Russ said, sliding the intricate
wrought iron door upward. His expression was as
grim as she felt.

She sighed and stepped into the cubicle, leaning
against the back wall. Russ gave a hard downward
yank, and the door clanged shut. He pressed the button for Logan's offices and the elevator began to lum-
ber upward, like an old man with creaking joints
ambling up a steep staircase.

Laura couldn't help noticing the tautness of Russ's
jaw as the lift toiled upward. She saw the color leech
from his cheeks when it stopped briefly with an un-
settling jerk before resuming its snail's pace. From
somewhere in her secret cache of memories came a

vague recollection of him telling her he was claustrophobic. She remembered laughing at the thought of big bad Russ Campbell being afraid of anything. She bit back a smile. Evidently, he'd been telling the truth.

The elevator ground to a stop, thankfully delivering them to their destination without mishap. It didn't take Russ more than five seconds to raise the door and step into the hallway, escaping the small enclosure.

"Who'd have ever believed it?" she asked with a wondering shake of her head.

"What?" he asked, but the look in his eyes said he knew what she was talking about.

"That Russ Campbell, tough guy, experienced roughneck, impromptu firefighter is scared of being cooped up in an elevator."

Dull color spread over his rugged features. "Yeah, well, we all have our Achilles' heel, don't we?" He gestured toward the office door. "After you."

With a smug smile, Laura swept past. Logan, dressed as casually as they were, waited for them in his office. He glanced at his watch as they stepped through the door. "On time. That's a first."

"Give it a rest," Russ said, pulling out a leather wing chair.

"Sure." Suddenly all business, Logan pulled a manila folder from a stack resting on the corner of his desk. He flipped it open and drew the top papers from it, glancing at them and then passing them to Laura. "This is the original of the joint custody papers. You and your attorney have looked at it?"

"Yes."

"Any problems?"

"No," she said. "My lawyer says the terms are more than fair."

"Good. Judge Bentley—a family friend—has already signed them."

Bemused, Laura leaned back in the chair, uncertain whether to be offended by the Campbells' collective colossal confidence or impressed with their ability to get things done.

They discussed the trust Russ had set up for Rufio, and Logan explained exactly what J.R. would inherit if anything happened to Russ. Laura was stunned.

"That's unbelievable," she said. It was hard to believe anyone had the kind of money they were talking about. "What about Jake and Zach? Shouldn't they get something from Gaspard Enterprises?"

"Mom has already taken care of that—not that Jake needs it." Logan grinned. "I imagine Zach will appreciate her generosity, though. The bulk of J.R.'s inheritance from Russ is his part of Campbell Drilling."

"Oh."

"Okay, the child support. Russ thought a couple hundred a week should be sufficient. Is that satisfactory?"

"A couple hundred a week?" Laura screeched, her shocked gaze moving from one Campbell brother to the other. "Are you kidding?"

"It isn't enough?" Russ asked, concern in his eyes.

"Enough! It's more than enough. I know women who get two hundred a *month*."

Relief skittered across Russ's features. "I want things to be easier for you."

"Well, another eight hundred a month should certainly do that," she said wryly.

Logan pulled a check free of a paper clip and handed it to her. "This is for the back child support."

Laura took the check, glanced at it and felt her mouth fall open. "I can't take this."

"Of course you can. He owes it to you."

"But this is almost fifty thousand dollars."

Laura listened attentively as Logan explained that the amount was the equivalent of two hundred dollars a week for the past five or so years of J.R.'s life—give or take a few weeks. She was left with the feeling that if she'd made a fuss or shown any sign of disappointment, Logan would have gotten out his trusty calculator and a calendar and figured the back child support to the day and the dollar.

"It doesn't seem right somehow."

"It's right," Russ said. "You can do what you want with it. Move to a bigger place."

She was pleased he'd said bigger—not better. "No," she said with a shake of her head. "That isn't my money. It's Rufio's."

Russ shrugged. "Fine. Then you can put it in some sort of savings, or Logan can look into investing it for you."

"I need to think about it."

"Sure," Logan said with an understanding smile. He gathered the papers and made some notes on the cover of the file.

"Is that it?" she said.

"That's it. Time to party. Well, almost."

"What?" Russ asked. "You aren't trying to get out of this, are you?"

"Of course not. But I've got to look up something, and I need to dictate some things for my secretary to take care of first thing in the morning. You two go on. I'll be about thirty minutes behind you.''

"Bliss will be furious."

Logan offered a wry smile. "She'll have to get used to it."

"Okay, then, we'll see you later."

"Yeah."

Placing a hand in the small of her back, Russ ushered Laura out of the office.

"I don't know what to say," she told him.

"About what?"

"Oh, come on, Russ," she said, casting him a stunned look over her shoulder. "You must know that this unexpected generosity of yours is mind-blowing stuff."

"It shouldn't be. If it helps any, think of it as penance."

"Penance?"

He nodded. "Reparation for all the times I wasn't there for him...and you. I know it can't make up for that, but it's the best I can do."

The expression in his eyes was one of genuine sorrow. Her heart spasmed in sudden pain. Why hadn't she realized before that coming to grips with this situation was as hard for him as it was her and J.R.? Hadn't all the interviews she'd done to prepare for writing her article taught her anything about the pain and sorrow of parent-child separation?

He raised the cage door of the elevator and gestured for her to precede him. Laura stepped inside.

"Don't do this to yourself," she told him as he pulled the door down. "It was never my intention to lay a guilt trip on you."

"I know. It was never your intention to tell me

about him.'' The words held no venom, only the sting of conviction.

She leaned back, her hands pressed against the side wall of the elevator, her rump resting on her hands. She wasn't aware that the posture thrust the fullness of her breasts against the soft brushed fabric of her shirt, but she was aware of the intensity of Russ's steady gaze.

''Even if I hadn't found out that J.R. had a heart condition, I would have told you about him. Working on the adoption article made me see how devastating hiding the truth can be. Seeing how much it hurt Jake to find out he was adopted and how he and Zach struggled with the question of who fathered them made me realize that even though I did what seemed right at the time, I was depriving both you and J.R. of something special.''

Russ nodded, as if her answer satisfied him, and pushed the button for the lobby. The elevator creaked downward. His gaze, moving as slowly as the old machine, drifted from her face over her breasts and down her body. A warmth she hadn't felt in ages pervaded her, thawing the chill that had surrounded her for so long, scattering her thoughts, leaving her feeling defenseless in the tumult of an increasing awareness. The elevator jerked. She hardly noticed.

''I almost went crazy when you left me.''

His confession stole her breath and caused her heart to throb in a hard and painful cadence.

''It was hell waking up every morning and finding the pillow next to me empty. I couldn't work. Hardly slept. I was so dangerous at the rig, Dad made me take some time off.''

Her throat thickened it with a swell of emotion so

strong it threatened to suffocate her. She shook her head. "Don't."

"Why?" he asked, in an exasperated voice. "We need to talk about it. I do, anyway."

The elevator lurched and shivered downward. She didn't want to talk about it. She was afraid that talking would soften her heart even more, and getting soft where Russ Campbell was concerned was hazardous to her heart.

"It won't change things. It won't—"

The elevator gave a squeal and a violent shudder. Paling, Russ muttered a curse. Then the elevator lurched and began to plummet downward. With a terrified squeal, Laura threw herself at him in an instinctive gesture of survival and solace. His arms closed around her, dragging her close, pushing her into the corner as his body curved protectively around hers. She was uttering a silent prayer when the ancient contraption jerked to a standstill with a snap that brought to mind the cracking of a whip.

For a moment, she was too petrified to move. Every nerve ending stood at attention. The remnants of terror magnified every sense. She could taste it in the dryness of her throat as she struggled to swallow. The stiffness and the fear left her by slow increments. She felt the trembling of her muscles reciprocated in the shudder that rippled through Russ.

She heard the harshness of his breath in her ear, felt its moist heat and the prickle of his whiskers against her jaw. He started to pull away. Her nails dug into his back, and she whimpered in denial, loath to lose the comfort of his nearness.

She heard him suck in a breath of surprise, felt him grow still and unmoving against her. He slid one hand between her shoulder blades, the other to the small of her back. Unlike the impersonal way he'd guided her from Logan's office, his touch, as he pressed her against him, was a combination of tenderness and repressed urgency.

The mind was a funny thing, she mused, as she clung to him, dreading…longing for his next move. She thought she remembered everything about him—the way the hair curled at the nape of his neck when it grew too long, the way his eyes crinkled at the corners, the way mischief danced in their amber depths when he smiled. But she'd forgotten how wide his shoulders were, how solid the wall of his chest felt against her cheek and how his six foot plus height dwarfed her, making her feel small and precious, cherished.

He'd forgotten how tiny she was, Russ thought, as Laura pressed against him, terror fusing their bodies the way passion once had. Forgotten the way her hair smelled, some exotic floral fragrance that whispered of ocean waves licking along a sand-strewn shore, of coconut palms and piña coladas and bougainvillea dripping scarlet blossoms.

He'd forgotten, too, the way she curled into him and how her head fit just so into the crook of his shoulder. But most of all, he'd forgotten how she made him feel. Big. Strong. Intensely masculine and acutely alive.

Driven by the looming specter of death—a bequest of his childhood heart condition—he'd determined at a young age to wring the very most from every minute of his life. Laura, with her desire to get at the facts and her need to make a place for herself in the world, was his flip side.

Without knowing it, her enthusiasm for perfection in whatever she did had shown him the importance of focus and maintaining a sense of self in the teeming, scheming world, while her passionate approach to life and love had taught him not to settle for second best, which is why, he now realized, he'd never married. No one had come close to making him feel what she did. And he knew now that no one ever would.

Threading his hand through the thickness of her hair, he tipped her head until she was forced to meet his eyes. She slicked her tongue over her lips, leaving them dewy wet and irresistible.

Without thinking of repercussions, needing only to reacquaint himself with the sweet promise he saw in her eyes, he kissed her, taking her mouth with a hungry savagery that surprised them both. Laura met that fierceness with an urgency of her own, taking his probing tongue deep inside her mouth while she pressed closer and closer still....

She couldn't get close enough. Even as the thought danced through her mind, she felt Russ's hands cup her bottom and lift her so she was wedged between the weight of his body and the wall of the elevator.

The hardness of him pressed against her brought a profusion of memories. Another whimper escaped her caused not by fear, but by need running amok. She wanted to rip off her blouse, to tear the buttons from his shirt and feel the crispness of his chest hair against the sensitive, aching tips of her breasts.

She was thinking crazy...if she was thinking at all,

but she didn't care. It had been so long since she'd felt anything like this, so long since she'd felt....

She felt his hand between them, working at the snaps of jeans, dragging down zippers, sliding denim over her hips and his. With a skill that left her breathless, his nimble fingers skimmed the impediment of silk, breaching the flimsy barrier of elastic that guarded the treasure he sought.

His mouth abandoned hers, leaving her lips naked and bruised. He nudged aside her collar and buried his lips in the hollow where her neck and shoulder met, lifting her and joining them with a ruthlessness that left no doubt of the depth of his need.

With a gasp of intense pleasure, Laura opened herself to him and the love she knew she'd never stopped feeling.

Her hands moved restlessly over his face, his hair, his shoulders. Her lips covered the side of his jaw with hungry little kisses until he tired of her games and fastened his mouth to hers again, matching the pace of his thrusting tongue with the movements of his body. Just when she thought she would go insane with the need for satisfaction, he gave a low cry of release and sent her spinning into a shimmering, glittering sea of sensation where time stood still and gratification washed over her in sweeping, gigantic waves.

Laura didn't know how long they stood there bound together in flesh and spirit. The only thing she was aware of was the slowing beat of her heart and the pulse in Russ's neck beating strongly against her lips.

For the first time in six years, she felt whole, at peace.

"Russ!" Logan's voice, worried and hollow-sounding, came from somewhere above them. "What happened?"

Russ drew back enough that he could look her in the eyes. "Damned if I know," he said to Laura, his voice as bewildered as she felt.

To Logan, he yelled, "Your stupid elevator broke. I think we're stuck between floors."

Logan's curse drifted to them. "Are you okay?"

Russ smiled, a naughty, lopsided smile that snatched her breath. "Never better," he shouted.

"The repair crew should be here soon. Jeez, Russ, I'm sorry. I know how paranoid you are about being in small places."

"It's okay," Russ called, blessing Laura with another slow stroking motion that warned her he wasn't finished with her yet. Just before he kissed her, he whispered, "I think I've found a cure for claustrophobia."

It was more than half an hour before the repairmen arrived. By that time, Laura, who'd been thoroughly and completely loved, stood in one corner of the elevator, her arms crossed over her breasts, her head turned away from Russ, her face a mask of confusion and mortification.

Russ lounged in the opposite corner, regarding her thoughtfully, like a cat who had cornered a mouse and was trying to figure out which way and when the critter was going to bolt.

Neither spoke. What had happened between them had been so basic, so elemental, it needed no discussion. The problem wasn't what had happened—it was what would happen next. Russ wasn't sure either of them had a clue how their spontaneous sexual encounter might alter their already shaky relationship.

She couldn't say he had forced himself on her, so any anger she might be feeling should be directed at herself. *Should.* But what should be and what was often tended to be two different things, as life had already taught her.

She glanced at him. His frown deepened. She was looking at him as if he were Jack the Ripper, for cryin' out loud!

"Hey!" The booming voice came from above them. "You okay down there?"

"Yeah!" Russ called. "Fine." But he wasn't fine, and he suspected Laura wasn't, either.

"Good. Press the start button, and let's see what happens."

His gaze met Laura's. The look in her eyes asked if she should do as the voice said. Remembering the elevator's dizzying dive, he understood exactly where she was coming from.

"We're not going to fall into the basement and break every bone in our bodies, are we?" he shouted through hands cupped around his mouth.

The question was answered by a rough, grating laugh. "There ain't no basement, buddy. What happened was a pulley gear slipped. I got it all fixed. You're about five feet from the lobby. If you fall, all you'll get's a sprained ankle." The prediction, an attempt to lighten the moment, was followed by another jarring chuckle.

Neither Russ nor Laura laughed, but he felt the same relief he saw on Laura's face rush through him. It was funny that he'd taunted death most of his life, but this most recent encounter had shown him he wasn't so anxious to cash in his chips after all. There was still a lot of living he wanted to do. And, he thought, his gaze raking Laura again, a lot of loving.

He nodded, and she pressed the red button. The elevator started downward without so much as a wobble, delivering them to their destination in seconds.

Logan, who'd taken the stairs, stood waiting for them, a look of concern on his face. He reached down and flung the gate upward as soon as the cubicle came to rest.

"You okay?" he asked, his troubled gaze moving from Russ to Laura and back again.

"Just dandy, thanks," Russ snarled as Laura brushed past them and pushed through the double doors that led to the sidewalk. Russ punched his brother in the chest with his index finger. "Ambience be damned. Get the elevator replaced before that happens to someone who'll slap a lawsuit on you."

With that bit of brotherly advice, Russ followed Laura outside.

"I need to go to the house."

"But breakfast—"

"They can eat without us. I need some time..." She shrugged. "A shower."

"It won't wash off, Laura. You can't ignore what happened. We need to talk about this."

"Not now, Russ," she said, turning and starting toward his truck.

He caught up with her in a couple of running steps and grabbed her arm. "When?"

She turned on him so fast it caught him by surprise. "I don't know!" she cried in a fierce, angry whisper. "Now are you going to take me to the house or do you want me to catch a cab?"

He regarded her for a long second. "I'll take you."

Russ worked his fingers into the pocket of his jeans. The soft denim pulled snugly across his sex. A soft, indrawn breath hung on the morning air. He drew the keys out and handed them to her. They were warm. Her fingers were cold. "Go on to the truck. I'll tell Logan we'll meet them at the Superdome."

She nodded, and Russ watched her walk away with a sinking feeling in his heart. Where, he wondered, thrusting a hand through his hair, did they go from here?

The remainder of the day taught Laura one thing—she was a better actress than she'd ever imagined. She and Russ hardly spoke during the ride to the house. They went up the broad, curving stairway in silence. At the top of the steps, when she was about to go one way and he the other, he had put his hand on her shoulder.

Startled by the sudden contact, she spun to face him, her eyes wide and wary.

"This doesn't have to change things," he said.

Madré de Dios! How could he even think such a thing, much less say it? It changed *everything*.

"Still as sensitive as you always were, huh, Russ?" she said. She shook off his hand and headed toward her room.

"Laura?"

She whirled, the movement so fast it brought a look of disbelief to his rugged features. "Give it a rest, okay?"

He nodded. When she got to the door of her room, she cast him a sideways glance and saw that he still stood where she'd left him.

As she showered, she tried to make some sense of what had happened. Heat suffused her body that had nothing to do with the steaming water cascading from the shower head. Had she really made hot, passionate love with Russ in a stalled elevator, standing up and with her clothes on?

Yeah, she had.

What bothered her was why. There was no use denying she loved him, which made her actions even more ludicrous. With their history, she'd been a fool to tip her hand by letting him touch her. Hadn't she learned the hard way that he had little use for what he gained too easily? She groaned, knowing she'd messed up royally, knowing, too, that there was no easy way out of the path she'd chosen.

When she made her way downstairs thirty minutes later, freshly showered and changed, he was waiting for her, pacing the elegant living room and tapping a rolled-up newspaper against his palm. She saw that the reddish highlights in his hair were dimmed with dampness. He must have showered, too.

"I called Mom's cell phone and told her we're on our way."

"Good."

He thrust the newspaper toward her. "Here's the Dallas paper. I went out and got you a copy while you were getting ready."

Surprised—and touched—that he remembered, she took the paper with a muted thanks.

She started to open it, but Russ glanced at his watch and said, "Want to have a look at that in the truck? We need to be on the way."

"Sure!" she said. "No problem."

She looked over the article on the way to the Superdome, her eyes moving rapidly over the print and accompanying photos. Finally, realizing that her thoughts were more focused on the tight-lipped man beside her than the words she'd researched and written with such care to detail and honesty, she folded the paper and put it in her lap.

Russ must have heard her sigh. "I read it. It's good. No, it's better than good. You're a great journalist, Laura."

She knew her surprise at his praise must be reflected in her eyes. "Thanks."

Conversation between them died a quiet death. She was thankful when they reached the stadium and were caught up in the excitement of the game and answering the dozens of questions about their near miss in the elevator.

J.R. beamed, thrilled by the whole scenario—from the size of the Superdome to the fact that all he had to do was mention he wanted something and either Russ or Logan's wallet came out of a hip pocket. They were spoiling him, but Laura was too concerned with her own problems to care.

She recalled none of the game, little of their goodbyes to Russ's family. She did remember Russ lifting J.R. into the plane and helping her up, and she had a vivid image of the uncertainty in his eyes as he'd said, "I'll call."

Seeing that Bliss's feminine intuition had picked up on the new thread of tension between her and Russ and was working overtime on what might have caused it, Laura took the coward's way out and feigned sleep during the flight to Dallas. At the airport, Bliss helped load the suitcases and buckled J.R. into the front seat.

"Thanks," Laura said, impulsively embracing

Bliss in a sisterly hug. "I appreciate your flying us home. I know you must be exhausted."

"No problem. I love flying."

"Be careful going back."

"Always," Bliss said, shoving back a swath of platinum hair, a saucy grin on her wide mouth.

Laura was getting into the driver's seat when Bliss said, "Laura!"

"Yes?"

"Cut yourself some slack."

"What?"

"Whatever happened between you and Russ in that elevator—and I know something did—don't go placing blame on yourself or him. Take it for what it was and go from there."

Chapter Ten

Not because he really believed in them, but out of a habit he'd picked up from Regina, the first thing Tom Barnette read when he got the newspaper was his horoscope. Since it was located in the same section of the paper, he couldn't help but see Laura Ramirez's article, "Adoption—Then and Now," on the section's front page.

He read the piece with grim determination, uncertain whether he hoped to glean something of importance from it or if he was satisfying his curiosity. He put the paper down having reached one conclusion. Whatever else she was, the woman could write.

Her interviews with the people she'd talked to painted a vivid picture of facts, figures and procedure from adoptions in the past as well as today. But she'd done something else. She'd managed to capture the many and varied emotions connected to giving up a child—from women who had given up babies, their boyfriends and parents, as well as the children who'd been given up.

She'd supplied a gripping overview that provided just enough information to pique interest and guarantee readership in the detailed articles to follow. Tom knew he'd be reading.

Ever since Ben Lattimer had called a few months back to tell him about the appearance of Jake's unknown brother, Tom had spent more time than he liked thinking about babies.

The more intricate the development became, the more convinced Tom grew that something *had* happened that night, something Lilli hadn't told him about. Something that, if the media connected it to him in any way, would destroy his chance at the polls. Another accusation of wrongdoing was the last thing he needed since Logan Campbell was aiding and abetting the attorney general's office in an all-out effort to bring him down.

"I had an interesting call this afternoon."

What was it about the best laid plans? Tom took one look at his wife's set features and forgot about going to see Lilli. Regina was in one of her moods, and he was in for a rough evening.

Besides worrying about switched babies, he'd had one heck of a day—speeches, meetings, a press conference where he tried once more to beat back the flame of controversy surrounding his part in the Aegean Insurance scandal, and last but not least, another row with Ashlie, who again tried to exact a promise that he'd divorce Regina as soon as the votes were counted—no matter what the outcome.

Politician that he was, he'd pacified her as best he could without committing to anything that might come back to haunt him. When he'd left her, she'd been quiet, not ranting and raving and making threats the way she did so often, so he thought she believed him. Regina's ambiguous statement about receiving an interesting phone call made him question that belief.

"What kind of call?"

"Oh, just a chatty little talk, girl to girl, you know, between me and your mistress. Ashlie, isn't it?"

Tom's heart sank as his ire rose. Ashlie had threatened to call before, but he'd always managed to placate her. This time he'd failed, and she'd made good on her threat. Damn the little witch! When he saw her, he'd wring her beautiful neck.

It was one thing for a man to have a suspicious wife, another for that man's wife to be contacted by his current mistress. With the election less than two weeks away, he didn't need to lose the support of Regina and her family, scions of Fort Worth society who'd been involved in Texas politics since the Alamo.

"Look, Regina, I don't know what she said, but I assure you, it isn't what it seems."

"Really?" she said coldly. "Well, what it seems is that you've been keeping this Ashlie person in an expensive town house for several months now, promising her that you'd leave me and marry her as soon as the election is over."

"I never said—"

"Please, Tom," Regina said, silencing him with an upheld palm and an icy look. "Don't try to deny it. I've known about her—just not her name—for weeks.

We both know she isn't the first. She's just lasted the longest.''

"Regina, I don't know what to say.''

"There's nothing you can say, so salvage whatever pride you have by not stooping to lies. And if you have no pride, then have the decency to spare me the sight of your groveling.''

Shocked into silence, Tom stared at his wife, the mother of his thirty-eight-year-old daughters, the woman who'd slept at his side and stuck by him through thick and thin, wondering how he could have been married to her for forty years and never have seen this steely side of her.

Maybe you were seeing it all along, Tom, old buddy, and just didn't recognize it. Tom had a sneaking suspicion the taunting voice was speaking the truth.

"So I'm caught with my pants down, huh?'' he asked with a nervous laugh, picturing a future without Regina at his side. Not liking that image at all.

"Caught with your pants down.'' A wry smile claimed her mouth. "That's as good a way of putting it as any. I'll give your Ashlie this, though. She has more guts than the others.''

Regina gave a negligent shrug. "Maybe it's best she called. I planned on having it out with you, anyway, but I thought I'd wait to confront you after the election and the Aegean Insurance mess blew over.''

"I'll end it, Gina,'' he said. "Ashlie has become far too demanding, and—''

"Don't end it on my account.'' She sighed. "I'm tired of the women in your life. I'm tired of being talked about behind my back. I'm tired of the pity, but mostly, Tom, I'm tired of not having a decent man in my life.''

Tom saw the hurt in her eyes, the sheen of tears, the tatters of her pride. A small but sharp pain, like a pinprick to the finger, stabbed through him.

''It might have escaped your notice, Tom, but I'm attractive. And I'm well kept, for my age.'' She laughed, a bitter sound that held no trace of humor. ''There have actually been a couple of men who thought I was sexy.''

Tom felt his face stiffen in shock.

She laughed again, and this time her lips curved in a smug smile. ''Does it surprise you that I've had opportunities, too, Tom? How naive of you. The difference is, I never acted on them. The vows I took all those years ago meant something to me.''

She squared her shoulders. ''I've never betrayed you, Tom, because somehow I managed to stay a fairly decent person in spite of our life in politics. But I realized something recently. I deserve more from life than what I've had with you. And I deserve better than you.''

His voice was a hoarse whisper. ''Regina, please. What are you saying? What are you going to do?''

She laced her fingers together, raised her chin and looked down her patrician nose. ''Move my things to the guest room, for starters. From there, I honestly don't know.''

Tom watched her leave the room. Calling Lillian Hampstead was the last thing on his mind.

Laura wasn't prepared for the overwhelming response to the article. Letters were faxed and calls were made to the newsroom by people who'd been involved in adoptions in some way. Her editor declared the series an unqualified success on the strength of one day's response, and the television station that had been courting her called and wanted another meeting to discuss added perks.

She was at her desk, basking in the glow of her triumph, her encounter the day before with Russ momentarily forgotten, when someone yelled that she had a phone call.

"I'm busy!" she said. "Get a number."

"No dice. This woman insists on talking to you, preferably now."

Sighing, Laura picked up her extension adopting her most professional voice. "Laura Ramirez."

"Ms. Ramirez, my name is Barbara Cauthon. Several weeks ago, I responded to your ad for people who'd been involved with adoptions, especially young girls who'd been sent to a home for unwed mothers." The voice was sharp, nervous.

Cauthon. There was something familiar about the name, but Laura couldn't put her finger on it. She stifled a yawn. Memories of her encounter with Russ in the elevator had robbed her of the better part of a night's sleep.

"Normally I wouldn't bother you, but when you mentioned the home in Brownsboro, I just had to call."

For the first time since she had picked up the phone, Laura's attention was piqued. There had been a couple of people she was supposed to interview, but J.R.'s tests had forced her to cancel. What Laura found interesting was that it was the mention of the home in Brownsboro that caught Barbara Cauthon's attention.

Originally, Laura had no plans to use the mix-up—and still didn't, as far as delving into details and names. But the more she'd thought about it, the more convinced she'd become that reporting the sometimes lackadaisical and prejudicial attitudes of the people who dealt with these young women was a vital part of the adoption experience, one that often left a legacy of guilt the women lived with for the remainder of their lives.

Because that attitude often manifested itself in carelessness in the supervision and care of the babies, Laura had made passing mention of the incident she'd become involved with through Zach Rawlings. Out of deference to her employer, who frowned on the possibility of lawsuits, she had in no way connected the switch with Lillian's home for pregnant teens or the Brownsboro hospital.

"I was at the home in Brownsboro," Barbara Cauthon said.

Her voice trailed away, as if she were having trouble finding her next words, but the simple statement was enough to jog Laura's memory. Barbara Cauthon's letter was the one mentioning Brownsboro she'd told Zach about when he came to her and told her he was considering finding out more about the night of his and Jake's birth. The importance of that connection had slipped her mind as she tried to balance work and worry with Rufio's bouts of sickness and innumerable trips to various doctors.

"Yes, Mrs. Cauthon. I remember now. I had to cancel our appointment."

"Yes."

"I'm so sorry," Laura apologized, "but my little

boy has been having some health problems, and I just never seemed to find the time to get back to you.''

''It's all right. Like I said, I wouldn't bother you, except that you mentioned Brownsboro, and—'' She broke off and Laura heard her take a deep breath, as if she were trying to stockpile air before plunging into the deep end of the pool. ''Look, if you're looking for a story about wrongs to unwed mothers, I can fill your ear about the home in Brownsboro.''

Wrongs. Brownsboro. Barbara Cauthon had uttered the magic words. If this woman knew anything about Lillian's operation, no matter what it was or when it had happened, Laura wanted to hear it, and told her so. She made arrangements to meet her that evening.

Barbara Cauthon was thin, nervous and, as Laura had learned via the phone, short and sarcastic. The first words out of the now almost-sixty-year-old woman's mouth after she and Laura sat down to coffee at the small kitchen table were, ''Lillian Hampstead was a bitch.''

Laura's eyes widened in surprise. An interesting viewpoint, since Tom Barnette had extolled the octogenarian's virtues. ''What do you mean?''

''Just that,'' Barbara said, her expression thoughtful. ''A bitch and a looker.''

She was silent for long seconds, lost in the bitter tangle of her memories. When the minutes ticked by and she still didn't speak, Laura said, ''Barbara?''

Barbara lit a cigarette and drew on it deeply, then blew a stream of smoke toward the ceiling. ''Lillian Hampstead had a body made for G-strings and tassels, not a white uniform. And she had the most gorgeous auburn hair I've ever seen. As far as looks, she had it all, the whole enchilada, you know? But she had the personality of a cobra.''

She met Laura's surprised gaze, her eyes glittering with tears. ''I was sixteen when I got pregnant. Sixteen and scared to death. I wanted to keep my baby, but my parents said I had to adopt it out, so I went to stay at Lillian's place.''

She shook her head and brushed at her eyes. ''I remember them signing some papers. I was embarrassed and nervous. Daddy carried in my suitcase, then he and Mama hugged me, got in their car and left. I still remember thinking that they were relieved that I was out of their hair, you know?''

Laura nodded, but she *didn't* know. When she'd told her parents she was pregnant with Russ's child, she'd known they were disappointed and heartsick, but they'd never made her feel unloved or unwanted.

''We were all so young and scared,'' Barbara continued. ''We knew we'd messed up big-time. We'd thrown away our innocence, and we were paying for our stupidity. A kind word would have gone a long way. A hug or a shoulder to cry on would have been nice, but what we got was that we should have listened to our parents or been more careful. You reap what you sow. If you want to dance, you have to pay the fiddler—that sort of garbage. If we wanted sympathy, we had to get it from Ruthie.''

Ruthie. Bells went off inside Laura's head just as they had when Lillian had mentioned the name, but this time the clamor was louder, and this time she knew why. Ruthie was the name of the woman Georgia had told her about the day at the ranch. The woman whose interview Laura had turned down because she had enough information for the article. The woman Lillian had mentioned. Laura felt a rising sense of excitement. Could she finally be getting a much-needed break? If she could find this good woman, maybe she could tell her something about Abby Pickett's lover.

"Ruthie?" she asked Barbara.

"Yeah, she was the housekeeper and cook. She was a nice lady."

"Do you remember her last name?"

"Not offhand," Barbara said. "Sorry."

"It's okay," Laura assured her. She'd give Georgia a call as soon as she got home and check out the connection.

"Maybe Lillian didn't mean to be callous," she said to Barbara. "Maybe she was just trying to get her point across, to make you see that you should be more careful in the future. I'd think the kind of person who'd choose to run a facility for unwed mothers would be someone concerned about the welfare of both the mother-to-be and the baby."

Barbara Cauthon laughed, a sound that held more bitterness than mirth. "Concern? Lillian? Boy, are you wrong. She did it because she liked money, honey."

"Money?" Laura echoed. "Those places weren't money-makers. They struggled to get by on the pittance they got from the state and charitable donations."

Barbara reached for her cigarettes. "This wasn't a state-run facility, Ms. Ramirez. You didn't stay there for free, let me tell you."

Again, the news caught Laura off guard. How could she have been so stupid as to assume the home was state-run? She'd never once considered that it was privately owned and operated. "You paid to stay there?"

"Damn straight. And it was pricey, even back then. I still remember my dad griping about it." She took a drag from the cigarette and drew the smoke deep. "Lillian drove a fancy car. A Cadillac convertible. That ought to tell you something."

Laura hardly heard. She was too busy going from pricey to preacher and wondering how a poor country minister could afford to send his daughter to Lilli Hampstead's home.

Barbara wiggled her fingers, drawing Laura's attention. "She had a different ring for every day of the week. And when she wasn't at the hospital, she dressed to the nines. It took money to support the lifestyle she lived."

Laura remembered the rings that had flashed on Lillian Hampstead's skinny fingers with a sinking heart.

"Maybe her husband was well off," she suggested, not wanting to believe the old woman with the failing memory and bright smile was as greedy and coldhearted as Barbara Cauthon depicted her.

"She was divorced." Barbara tapped a length of ash into the ashtray. Her mocking gaze found Laura's. "She did have a boyfriend, though. *He* was married."

Laura shifted uncomfortably. She prided herself on her professionalism, and this was quickly becoming a gossip session. "I understand your disenchantment with Lillian Hampstead and your stay in Brownsboro, but charging for a much-needed service—even overcharging to live the good life—isn't a crime. What you've told me might be wrong morally, and it will bring a few tears to the readers' eyes, but my editor wants facts, not feelings.''

Barbara stubbed out her cigarette. ''You want a story, huh? Well, that's what I promised you, so here goes. By the time my baby was due, I'd made up my mind to keep it, whether my parents liked it or not. They didn't, but they finally agreed to let me keep it if I'd go live with my aunt Patty in Detroit. Daddy was the president of the bank, and he didn't want anything to mar his sterling image with the public.

''When I went into labor, I was too dumb to know it was the real thing. By the time I got around to calling Lillian at the hospital, she said I'd waited too long and we shouldn't risk the trip. She delivered the baby right there at the home.''

''You had your baby without anesthetic?''

Barbara shook her head. ''She gave me a shot of some kind. Said the doctor had given her leeway to administer it if anything like this should come up. It made me groggy and knocked the edge off the pain.''

Laura barely hid her surprise. Valerie Campbell claimed Lillian had administered painkillers to her, too.

''Lillian told me my baby was born dead,'' Barbara said, as a single tear trickled down her cheek. ''She said the cord was wrapped around its neck.'' She wiped her eyes. ''Lord, I grieved for that little girl. I felt like God was punishing me for what I'd done.''

''That's ridiculous,'' Laura scoffed.

''I know that now, but it took years of counseling before I could think about it without feeling this overwhelming guilt, even though I knew in my heart of hearts Lillian had lied.''

"Why would she lie, Barbara?" Laura asked gently.

"For a smart lady, you're a little slow," Barbara said with a halfhearted grin. "Ever hear of black-market babies?"

For some reason she didn't understand, Laura's heart began to beat faster. "Of course I have. Are you telling me that you believe Lillian Hampstead told you your baby was dead so she could sell it to some-one and keep the money for herself instead of putting it up for adoption through legal channels?"

"That's exactly what I believe." Barbara lit an-other cigarette.

"Why?" Laura heard the relentlessness in her voice and hated herself for it, but these were serious accusations, accusations that would need backing up by more than the muddled, guilt-ridden feelings of a sixteen-year-old who'd received a painkiller.

"I heard her cry." Seeing the skepticism in Laura's eyes, Barbara continued. "I know, I know. I told you I was drugged up, so you probably think I imagined it, but I didn't.

"It was several weeks after Lillian told me my little girl was dead that I was back home, lying in bed, thinking about that night—how she made all the other girls go to their rooms, how she kept talking to me while she was delivering the baby. I was pretty much out of it. I remember that, but when she asked me something, I'd answer her, even though I might not remember what I said two seconds later. But I re-member hearing my baby cry. I've lived through my memories of that night a thousand times, and the more I do, the more sure I am. I know she was alive, be-cause I heard her cry."

"Barbara…"

"You don't believe me." She took a deep pull off the cigarette. "I can't blame you. And if it weren't for the fancy way she lived and the fact that her boyfriend handled all the adoptions, I might have believed the lie myself. As it was, it took me a long time to put it all together."

"Her boyfriend? The married man?" When Barbara nodded, Laura asked, "What did he have to do with the adoptions?" She felt uneasy.

"He was a lawyer. *Is* a lawyer."

Laura's heart began to beat faster. "I don't suppose you know who the man was?" she asked, wanting nothing more at that moment than to hear the answer, yet fearful of what it would be.

"Sure I do. Lilli's beau was none other than our esteemed senatorial candidate, good ol' Texas boy and all-around slimeball, Tom Barnette."

It had taken every bit of control Laura had not to betray the shock that coursed through her at Barbara's casual statement. Lillian and Tom had been lovers. No wonder he'd been so anxious to make her look good.

Until Barbara connected the personal lives of the adoption duo, Laura might have taken her claim of a stolen baby with a grain of salt. But when she put that information next to the fact that there was something amiss the night the Campbell boys were born, and Tom and Lillian had been involved with that, too, an ugly picture began taking shape.

Laura had believed that the mix-up was purely accidental. By all accounts the night had been chaotic. But now she wasn't so sure. She didn't have a clear picture of what had gone on, but she did know that Lillian lied to Abby and the Lattimers. What she didn't know was why.

To cover her tail, that's why.

But for what reason?

Laura worked her way through the facts. For the sake of argument, she'd assume Barbara was right and her baby had been stolen and sold to some wealthy couple so Lillian could enjoy the high life. Question number one, had she acted alone or had Tom been her accomplice? Question two, had the mix-up with Logan and Russ and Jake and Zach been part of one of her schemes? If so, how?

There'd been no mysterious baby death connected to their case, no parent robbed of a child the way Barbara Cauthon claimed. The Lattimer adoption seemed legal and aboveboard. Abby took the other child she believed was hers. The Campbells took home two babies, albeit not the right ones. So what had Lillian been trying to hide?

Maybe you're trying too hard to make her out a villainess when she isn't one. Maybe Barbara is imagining things.

Yeah, maybe, but doubtful. There were too many things that didn't add up. Laura could believe Lillian suffered from memory loss. After all, she was getting on in years. But that didn't alter the fact that Lillian had lied to her about having a nephew. Why? And if she'd lied about that, what else had she been untruthful about?

The first thing she did when she got home was call Georgia Rawlings and tell her about her latest information. She asked for Ruthie's last name and phone number, saying she hoped this Ruthie was the same one Lillian and Barbara had mentioned.

"As a matter of fact, I'm sure it is," Georgia said. "I'm positive Ruthie worked at the home in Brownsboro, which is why I thought you'd want to talk to her, but I also knew she wouldn't know anything about Zach because she didn't go to work for Lillian until eight years after that, so it was no big deal."

"Well, as it turns out it may be a big deal. I'm sorry I seemed so uninterested," Laura apologized. "It was a pretty stressful day, as I recall."

"Don't worry about it," Georgia said. "I'm just glad you're finally getting a break with this."

"Yeah, me, too," Laura said. She thanked her new friend and said goodbye. As soon as she'd broken the connection, she punched in the number she'd been given.

When Ruthie got on the phone and Laura explained that she was trying to investigate an allegation of Lillian Hampstead selling babies, the old woman said, "I always thought there might be something like that going on, but I never had any proof. To be quite honest, Ms. Ramirez, I quit because I had a bad feeling about that place. I felt guilty on the one hand, because I knew those young girls needed a shoulder to cry on, but in the end, I just didn't want to be a part of it—cousin or not."

"You and Lillian Hampstead are cousins?"

"Second cousins," Ruthie said. "Not that I'm proud of it, you understand. She always did put on airs and think she was better than the rest of us blood kin, but when I needed a job after Elton died, she took me in, so I guess she isn't all bad."

"But you think she was stealing babies. Why?"

"Maybe because there were nine that supposedly died the eighteen months I was there, and they all belonged to girls who'd changed their minds about giving their babies up."

"It does sound suspicious, doesn't it?"

"It does, indeed," Ruthie said.

"Did you ever confront her?"

"Confront Lillian? Are you kidding?" Ruthie gave a derisive snort. "Why, she'd have gouged out my eyeballs if I'd dared question anything she did."

"I understand she was having an affair with Tom Barnette."

"Yes, she was, and I did say something to her about that. She wasn't raised to be a home breaker, Ms. Ramirez. She didn't talk to me for two months, as I recall." Ruthie laughed. "At least I didn't have to put up with her constant criticism."

"If Lillian was involved in black-market babies, do you think Tom was involved?"

There was a thoughtful pause. "It's hard to say. He liked the finer things, too, but he didn't come around all that much. He seemed different then, somehow. I just don't know. I can't make a call on that one."

"Well, thanks, Ruthie," Laura said. "I appreciate the information."

"Certainly, honey, but what you really need is proof, isn't it?"

"Yeah," Laura said, "it is."

"I'm sorry I wasn't more help."

"Having you confirm this other woman's story is a great help," Laura told her.

"That's good, then, and by the way, the article is wonderful."

Laura thanked her again and hung up with a sigh.

As promising as it had seemed, her conversation with Ruthie was just another wild-goose chase, other than confirming there was something going on between Lillian and Tom.

Even without proof, Laura felt compelled to call Logan and tell him about her conversations with Barbara Cauthon and Ruthie Parker.

"When you consider that Barbara's story was more or less corroborated by Ruthie, you have to figure Lillian was into something pretty heavy. Then there's the mix-up with all you guys, her lies about her nephew, and the fact that her mother stayed in an exclusive nursing home. Not to mention all that jewelry."

"Hot damn, Laura," Logan cried. "I think we've finally come up with something to nail Tom's hide to the wall!"

"Tom's hide? Logan, I'm talking about Lillian Hampstead, not Tom Barnette."

"Yeah, but you know what they say, where there's smoke, there's fire. It's there. I feel it. Jeez, what a sweet setup they had." He laughed. "Just wait until this hits the papers. The people of this state won't vote him in as dogcatcher."

"Whoa, gringo," Laura said with a laugh. "My editor won't let me run this until I have some concrete facts."

"Then what are you doing on the phone, woman?" he said. "Get out there and dig a little deeper."

Chapter Eleven

"You're obsessed with the man," Russ told Logan when his brother passed on the information he'd learned from Laura.

"Well, at least I have the courage of my convictions!"

"What the hell's that supposed to mean?"

"It means that when I want something, I go for it. When there's something wrong, I try to fix it."

Russ crossed his arms over his chest and shifted his weight to one foot. He had a suspicion about where this particular conversation was headed. "Spit it out, Golden Boy. I'm no damned mind reader."

"I'm talking about you and Laura and J.R."

A wary look leaped into Russ's eyes. He uncrossed his arms and thrust his hands into his back pockets, cocking his chin to a defiant angle. "What about us?"

"You're crazy about the kid. It's also as easy to

see as the guilt on both your faces when you got off that elevator yesterday that you're nuts about Laura."

"You're the one who's nuts."

"I don't think so. I figure a little hanky-panky went on while you were stranded in there, and knowing how hardheaded you are, I suspect all you plan to do about it is sit around and hope she grants you absolution, or maybe wait and see if her resistance weakens and it happens again, instead of taking some sort of action to ensure it does."

"What kind of action?"

"Something simple and elemental," Logan explained with the patient attitude one might use with a learning-handicapped individual. "Like treating her really nice and suggesting there might be a chance of something permanent between you two."

Russ looked at Logan as if he were crazy. "Permanent? Are you talking marriage?"

"Duh?" Logan said in the current teen vernacular. "Of course I'm talking marriage. Isn't that the next logical step when you love someone and want to be with them and share their life?"

"I'm not cut out for marriage."

Logan laughed, a hearty laugh that brought a frown to Russ's face. "You've spouted that crap to the women in your life for so long, you're starting to believe it. The truth is you're scared spitless of putting your heart on the line. Scared you'll get hurt."

"I'm not scared of anything. I'm just an irresponsible, selfish son of a gun who can't sustain a lasting relationship."

"Irresponsible," Logan said with a nod, as he started pacing the room. Logan paced when he was upset. Russ sought answers at windows. "That's how you've managed to keep Campbell Drilling going almost single-handedly the past couple of years.''

Seeing Russ's surprise, Logan said, ''I knew Dad had pretty much turned the whole operation over to you. He told me. And you've done a damn fine job of it, brother.''

''I'm an insensitive jerk.''

Logan stopped in his tracks and smacked his palm against his forehead, as if he'd been struck by a thunderbolt of understanding. ''Yeah. I should have seen it for what it was.''

''What?''

''What you did for Laura and J.R. yesterday wasn't the behavior of a man who cared for two people at all, a man who wanted to try and make up for his past actions as best he could. You just did it to prove what an irresponsible, insensitive, selfish jerk you are, right?'' Logan's voice was laced with unmistakable sarcasm.

''When did you become my champion?'' Russ asked, frowning at his brother, wary disbelief in his eyes.

''Ever since I saw you with her and the boy at the Lattimer ranch. You're crazy in love with the woman, bubba,'' Logan said in a gentle voice. There was no use denying it, and they both knew it. He started pacing again.

''I know that whatever happened between you after Odessa was a real and vital part of your life. When the two of you split, it almost killed you. You haven't been the same since.''

''She ripped out my heart.''

''And you didn't hurt her?'' Logan asked.

When Russ looked surprised, Logan said, ''That's

the way it works. I'm starting to see that if you love someone, hurting each other happens on a regular basis. I don't know, maybe you do it *because* of that love. Maybe it's a constant test.''

"I don't know if I can survive it again," Russ said, giving Logan a rare glimpse of his vulnerability.

"So she hurt you, and you're afraid she'll do it again, so you won't even try to take this to another level. I know you. If she shuts you out—which I suspect she did—to think her own feelings through after whatever happened yesterday, you'll just pull farther away, and before you know it, you'll stop calling to talk to J.R. As a matter of fact, you haven't called tonight, have you?"

"It's late," Russ said, guilt gouging like a knife.

"Whatever." Logan shrugged and went on, but Russ knew he wasn't buying it. "Next thing you know, you'll be making excuses—ones you really believe—to not go see him, and pretty soon your relationship with your son will be you signing your name to the bottom of a check the first of every month."

He stopped in front of Russ and delivered the final, conclusive blow. "But maybe you're right and I'm wrong about who and what you are. Maybe you're more like our selfish, irresponsible, no-good scumbag of an unknown father than I'd like to believe."

Russ thought about what Logan had said for the better part of an hour. As usual, his brother was right. But he was scared, more scared than he'd ever been in his life.

Time to put up or shut up, bubba.

Russ crossed to the phone. Logan was right. It was now or never. Shaking as hard as he had been when he stepped off the elevator the day before, Russ reached for the phone.

Inez told her J.R. had gone to bed pouting because Russ hadn't called. At Laura's look of dismay, she'd amended the statement, saying that he finally did call, but J.R. had already fallen asleep.

The gratefulness Laura felt was almost overwhelming. She'd so feared that what she was thinking of as the elevator episode would color Russ's relationship with his son.

By the time he called the following evening, she admitted that she was afraid it might affect their relationship, too. Her eagerness and need to hear his voice were fast overtaking her mortification at what she'd allowed to happen.

He sounded a bit stilted, but she felt uncomfortable, too. When she told him she'd accepted the television job—but as an investigative reporter, not an anchor—he offered her congratulations, but she sensed a reservation in his attitude.

"I couldn't see myself sitting behind a desk, reading the news off a TelePrompTer," she told him.

"No, that isn't you," he said. "You like the excitement of the hunt."

He was right. It wasn't the paycheck for her. It was the thrill of tracing down rare and interesting tidbits and exposing the corruptness and injustices of the world that made getting up and going to work worthwhile. But the excitement of knowing she'd done her best, had roused the rabble, had made people laugh, cry and think didn't begin to compare with the thrill and satisfaction she'd felt in his arms.

"It isn't exactly what I'm looking for, but I guess

it'll do," she told him. Russ didn't ask for an explanation, and she didn't elaborate.

"When do you start?"

"Two weeks, but the big shots want me to have a celebration dinner with them tomorrow night."

"Sounds like they're really trying to make you feel like part of the team."

"It's nice to be wanted."

As soon as the words left her mouth, she wanted to call them back. The last thing she needed was to remind Russ of Sunday.

"You're right," he said, his voice a low and intimate rumble, "it is."

"Russ—"

"I guess Inez is baby-sitting."

"As a matter of fact, she isn't. One of her kids has a musical program at school. I'm going to have to find someone."

"I'll come over and stay with him."

The offer, coming straight out of the blue, took her by surprise. "You have a business to run. I know I've questioned how much you're willing to be involved in Rufio's life, but I don't expect you to rearrange your schedule to come and baby-sit."

"I don't mind. I'd like to do it. I sense a softening in his attitude toward me."

"He doesn't hold grudges," she said.

"Unlike his mother."

"I don't hold any grudges over what happened between us six years ago, Russ, surely you now that by now."

"What about what happened between us Sunday?"

The boldness of the question made her breath catch in her throat. "I don't hold any grudge over that, either," she told him, her voice little more than a whisper.

"Then why aren't we talking about it?"

"I...I don't know what to say. It happened. It shouldn't have."

"I'm not sure I agree. Maybe we can't think of anything to say because our hearts said it for us."

Laura laughed, a soft expulsion of breath that sounded suspiciously like a sob. "I don't think that was our hearts. I think it was our bodies. I don't know about you, but it had been a long time for me."

"How long?"

She gave a gasp. "That's none of you business," she told him, but the statement lacked heat.

"How long?"

"Did anyone ever tell you you're egotistical, selfish and ruthless?"

"Yeah, you just did. How long, Laura?"

"Six years." She bit out the words angrily.

"Six years? You mean—"

"That's exactly what I mean. Now can we drop this, please?"

"Sure." Neither spoke for several seconds. Finally, Russ said, "What time should I be there tomorrow?"

"Inez leaves when I get home at five-thirty."

"I'll try to be there by noon, and give her the afternoon off."

"That isn't necessary."

"I know. But I want to."

"Fine," Laura said, her exasperation clear. "I'll see you then." She started to break the connection, but Russ's voice stopped her. "What?"

"I want to tell you that it hasn't been six years for me."

"As if I didn't know that," she said with a sarcastic laugh.

"But I do want you to know it's been almost a year, that there haven't been hordes of women in my life, and that however many there were, none of them made me feel a tenth of what you do."

Laura sucked in a surprised breath. Her heart began to beat raggedly in her chest. "Why are you telling me this?"

"Because I think Sunday proves there's still plenty of feeling between us. I think we owe it to ourselves as well as J.R. to see if we can figure out what it is and just what we plan to do about it."

When Laura got home on Wednesday afternoon, the house was quiet. She took a quick look out the back door and saw J.R. and Russ in the small yard, playing catch.

"Never take your eye off the ball, and get your glove under it like this," Russ said, demonstrating the action to J.R. Then he threw an easy overhand pitch, which J.R. proudly caught. "That's it. Good."

Laura drew in a shaky breath, remembering Russ's parting words the night before and afraid to put much hope in them. The sight of the two of them together, punching their fists into their gloves and doing their male bonding thing, was one she could easily get used to.

"Hey, Rufio!" she called, giving him two thumbs up. "Looking good."

"Mom!" he said, throwing the ball to Russ and running toward her. She knelt, bracing herself for the weight of his body as he flung himself into her arms. Lifting him, she straightened and faced Russ.

"Hi," he said, smiling at her as he armed the perspiration from his face.

The high-voltage smile jangled her nerve endings. She felt like a sixteen-year-old facing the boy responsible for her first big-time crush. "Hi. How's he coming along?"

"He's got good hand-eye coordination and more strength than I expected."

"Good," she said, giving the child a hearty squeeze.

"What time is your dinner?" Russ asked.

"Seven."

He nodded. "I thought J.R. and I would have a pizza delivered."

"How did you know he liked pizza?"

"He's a kid, isn't he?" Russ smiled again. "Actually, Zach told me it was his favorite thing."

"Oh." They stood there, acutely aware of each other, exhilarated, fearful, tentative, trying to think of something to say, as J.R. looked from one of them to the other, as if he were trying to figure out what caused the tension he felt stretching between them.

"I'm thirsty," he said at last.

"Go on inside and get a drink, then," Laura said, setting him on the ground. He ran toward the house, and Laura was left to deal with her runaway feelings for the man standing in front of her, his hair damp from his exertions, perspiration glinting off the hair-dusted chest exposed by his partially unbuttoned shirt.

"I need to take shower," she said, gesturing vaguely at the house.

"I could use one myself. I don't suppose I could join you?"

The look in his eyes said far more than their brief

exchange of words. The smile she dredged up was as much of a surprise as her reply. "Not this time."

Without another word, she turned and started toward the house. She'd gone no more than three steps when she felt his hand on her shoulder. She turned, her heart beating wildly inside her chest.

He slid his palm across her collarbone to rest at the base of her throat, his touch as soft as an angel's kiss. He slipped his hand up to cup her cheek, dragging his thumb across her lower lip in a gentle caress. "When you get home," he said, "we're going to have a serious talk."

The expression in his eyes said he meant business. She swallowed and nodded. "Okay."

"Good." He lowered his head and pressed a kiss to her lips. It was strictly a no-frills, generic kind of kiss, just the sweet joining of his lips to hers for the briefest of seconds. Laura felt need rising inside her like steam in a pressure cooker over a hot fire. She broke away, drawing a trembling breath.

"Go on," he said. "Take your shower. This will wait. Your new boss won't."

As Laura stepped through the back door, she heard Russ tell J.R. to take his place. When he complained he was tired, Russ said, "Just a little longer. You're getting the hang of it."

Laura smiled. Rufio had wanted the chance to play ball. Well, by golly, he was getting it.

Despite the fact that he claimed he was tired, Russ forced J.R. to stay outside for a while after Laura—who looked stunningly gorgeous in a plum-colored silk sheath—left, telling him the fresh air and exercise were good for him. Since he'd almost had to drag him from in front of the television, Russ suspected J.R.'s weariness had more to do with the fact that he'd rather be watching the latest antics of Scooby Do than running around in the backyard sweating over catching Russ's next pitch.

"I can't play any more," J.R. said finally, throwing his glove onto the grass and collapsing beside it. "I feel sick."

At first, Russ thought the statement was another ruse, but after one look at the child's pale, pinched features he quickly changed his mind. "My heart hurts. It's going too fast," J.R. said, pressing a hand to his chest.

Fear reared its head inside Russ's chest. "Let's get you inside, buddy," he said, his heart racing. He bent to pick J.R. up, but instead of reaching for Russ, J.R. doubled over in the grass and began to vomit.

Russ did what he could, which wasn't much, and when the bout was finished, he gathered J.R. up, holding him close as he ran inside and dialed emergency, giving all the necessary information to the woman who answered his call for help.

The brief time they waited for the arrival of an ambulance was as close to a true-life nightmare as Russ ever wanted to encounter. Later, he would remember nothing but pacing the kitchen with J.R. in his arms, praying for help to hurry, praying for him to be all right, feeling an impossible impotence as J.R. announced he was going to be sick again. But the worst, the very worst was the all-consuming guilt that took root in Russ's soul when J.R. looked at him with wide, terrified eyes and whispered "I'm scared."

The two simple words ripped into his heart like the

talons of a giant bird. "I know, son," he said. "I'm sorry. The paramedics are on their way, okay?"

Rufio nodded and put his thumb into his mouth, something Russ had never seen him do before. Almost as if his words had brought it, the ambulance howled to a stop in front of the house. Russ rushed outside with his precious burden and watched as they hustled J.R. inside.

He climbed inside and took his place next to the child, knowing that what had happened was his fault. As the doors shut and the ambulance screamed down the street, Russ wondered how he could explain what had happened to Laura.

J.R.'s doctor waited at the emergency room and whisked the child off for a thorough examination. Russ stood in the middle of admissions, kneading the back of his neck and feeling strangely empty.

"Sir?" a pleasant woman behind a computer monitor asked. "Are you the little boy's father?"

"Yes."

"I need to ask you some questions for his paperwork."

"Sure," Russ said, "but I need to call his mother first."

The woman nodded, and Russ went to find a phone, dreading the call that would interrupt Laura's celebration dinner and most certainly put an end to whatever progress they'd made in their relationship.

"Russ?" she asked, a note of concern in her voice. "What is it? Is Rufio okay?"

"We're at the hospital," he said, mentioning a name that had become too familiar to her over the past few months. "He's had another attack."

"What? What happened?" she cried.

"We were playing ball and..." Russ's voice cracked. "Look, just get over here. I'll tell you about it when you get here."

Russ had just finished giving what information he could when Laura burst through the doors.

Part of him registered that she looked beautiful, but the thing that made the greatest impact on him was the terror in her dark eyes as she sailed across the room toward him, tears streaming down her cheeks. When she reached him, she raised her fists and hit his chest. "What have you done to him?" she cried. "What have you done to my baby?"

Ten minutes later, after Laura had seen for herself that J.R. was responding to treatment, she realized that her accusations against Russ had been completely irrational and most certainly uncalled for. Whatever happened, Russ would never knowingly or purposefully put J.R. in jeopardy.

She left the boy resting, comforted by the fact that she could take him home when he woke up, and went to apologize to Russ. The woman behind the desk said the gentleman had left soon after Laura had gone to be with Rufio. No, he hadn't said where he was going.

Laura felt a sob work its way up her throat and pressed her fingers against her lips to hold it back. She didn't bother trying to stop the tears. She didn't know where Russ had gone, either, but she knew him well enough to know that in all probability, he wouldn't be back.

When Russ left the hospital after making sure J.R. was okay, he got in his rental car and headed for the airport. He wasn't scheduled to fly out until the next day, but he managed to book a seat on a midnight flight to New Orleans. It was almost three when he drove into the Campbell Drilling yard and let himself into the trailer he and Bliss had shared. He unplugged the phone and fell across the unmade bed, weary to the bone but unable to sleep for the sound of J.R.'s voice bouncing off the walls of his mind. *I'm scared.*

Laura had been right. It took more than donating sperm to be a father. It took more than wanting to. Whatever it took, it was as plain as the fear on J.R.'s face that James Russell Campbell didn't have it.

Determined pounding roused Russ from the deep sleep he'd fallen into just as the pink fingers of dawn had poked through the drab gray of the eastern sky.

"Open up, Russ!" Logan cried, banging harder. "I know you're in there."

Russ pushed himself to his elbows and glanced at the clock on the cheap nightstand. Seven-thirty. What the sweet hell could Logan want with him at this hour? Russ swung his feet—still clad in sneakers— to the floor and went to unlock the door.

Logan took one look at him and said, "You look like hell."

"Well, we all can't be as pretty as you, now can we, Golden Boy?"

"Cut it out, Russ," Logan said, pushing his way inside. "What are you doing here, anyway?"

Russ scrubbed a weary hand down his whisker-stubbled cheek. "I live here, remember?"

"No, you stay here sometimes." He pinned Russ

with a determined look. "Laura called about an hour ago looking for you."

Russ felt the color drain from his face. "What did she want?"

"To talk to you, obviously."

"Is J.R. okay?"

"He's fine."

"Good." Russ turned away and maneuvered the few short steps to the cramped kitchen, swinging the refrigerator door open and examining the contents. He reached for a bottle of Evian Bliss had left behind, unscrewed the top and lifted the bottle to his lips.

"Laura wants you to call her. She wants to apologize for the things she said to you."

Fresh pain sliced through Russ's heart. "There's no need to apologize for the truth."

Logan expelled a harsh breath. "Don't blame yourself for something that wasn't your fault. It was—"

The sound of the plastic water bottle hitting the living room wall halted Logan's speech. A landscape tumbled to the floor. The sound of shattering glass was clearly audible. So was the sound of water gurgling onto the floor, making a puddle in the worn carpet.

"It *was* my fault, damn it!" Russ said, his quiet tone more lethal than yelling. "I told you I was irresponsible, and this proves it."

"What are you talking about?"

"With my usual unparalleled conceit, I thought I knew better than Laura how to bring up a son, but I don't know anything about being a father. If I hadn't been trying so hard to pull a Jack Campbell and toughen J.R. up, he'd have never had that spell. But I'm not Dad, Logan, and J.R. isn't me, and it isn't the same situation at all. He hasn't outgrown his condition the way I had. I pushed him too hard, and I might have killed him.''

"So this is it?" Logan asked, his shoulders lifting in a disbelieving shrug. "One little incident and you're just going to throw in the towel?"

Russ managed a wry smile. "Actually, until this happened, I was going to do what you suggested and see if Laura and I could work on our relationship, but last night proves what I knew all along."

"And what's that, besides the fact that you're a first-rate horses's ass?" Logan queried with quiet sarcasm.

"They're both better off without me."

Logan snorted.

"Laura said it herself. She was doing just fine until I came along. Now that she has child support and a better-paying job, she'll do even better."

Logan threw his hands into the air, as if he'd heard enough, which he had. "Are you finished playing the martyr?"

Russ turned away. Muttering an angry curse, Logan grabbed Russ's shoulders, spun him around and slammed him hard against the refrigerator door. He grabbed a handful of Russ's wrinkled shirt and shoved his face so close their noses were inches apart. Amber eyes shot sparks into amber eyes. Fury made Logan's breathing as harsh as his voice.

"Money and good jobs don't have anything to do with this. We're talking about being a father," he said from between teeth clenched as tightly as his fists on Russ's shirt. "We're talking about telling J.R. the things you did as a kid, so he'll have a clear picture of who he is. We're talking about establishing a relationship with him, doing things with him. Okay, maybe you did push him a little too hard, but that didn't bring on the attack.''

"Yeah, right."

Logan released his hold on Russ's shirt. "If you're hell-bent on placing blame on someone, put it on Inez," he said, taking a step backward. "When you came to relieve her at noon, she forgot to tell you to give him his medication."

Logan refused to leave until Russ agreed to call Laura and tell her they had no future together. Russ knew his brother was right, that he owed her and J.R. that much, but it didn't make the task any easier.

She picked up the receiver on the second ring. "Hello."

Her voice sounded breathless, as if she'd just run a block.

"Logan said you called," he said, without preamble.

She didn't say anything for the span of several heartbeats. "Yes," she said at last. "I wanted to let you know that Rufio is fine."

"That's good."

"I'm sorry for the things I said when I got to the hospital." Was it his imagination, or did he hear the threat of tears in her voice? "I know you'd never do anything to hurt J.R."

"But I did, Laura," he reminded her.

"It wasn't your fault. Inez forgot to tell you about his medicine. It was—"

"It doesn't matter. I should have known better than to push so hard. Will you tell him I'm sorry?"

Another lengthy silence stretched over the phone

lines. "He's asking to see you," she said at last. "Why don't you tell him yourself?"

"I'm not coming back, Laura," he blurted, determined to make his stance known. "You were right. I'm not cut out for the dad thing."

"I think you've done an excellent job of being his father." Her voice sounded wobbly, like a toddler taking its first tentative steps.

"Yeah, so excellent I almost killed him."

"You didn't almost kill him!" He heard her sigh, heard the resignation in her voice. "He's gotten used to you being part of his life the past couple of weeks, Russ," she said softly. "You'll break his heart if you don't come back, and I'm not so sure that isn't worse than causing him physical harm."

"He's young. He'll get over it. Logan and I did."

He heard her sigh again. It sounded defeated this time. "What about us, Russ?" she asked. "What about this thing we feel for each other that you wanted to talk about?"

"You'll get over that, too," he said. "We both will."

Chapter Twelve

The pain of Russ's rejection was so crushing that Laura called the paper and asked to have the day off, on the pretext that she needed to be with J.R. The truth was, she didn't think she could get through the day without bursting into tears, which wasn't exactly professional behavior for Dallas's journalistic darling. It didn't help her mood that the heavy rains that had started while J.R. was in the emergency room the night before showed no signs of letting up.

Determined not to let Russ Campbell get the best of her, she channeled her pain into anger—not at him, but at his attitude. She might have known he'd shoulder more than his part of the blame. Already running scared of a commitment, this gave him a good excuse to back off. Funny. She'd never had him pegged as a coward.

It isn't that, Laura, and you know it. It goes deeper

than the usual male-commitment phobia. It has a lot to do with his past, with being separated from his brother and his mother.

"It isn't about committing. It's about losing the people he loves," she said, understanding for the first time exactly where Russ was coming from, where he'd always come from. What he didn't seem to realize was that he was doing the same thing with J.R.

Knowing that the only way she could get through the day was to keep her normal routine, she ran into the downpour and got the paper. Inside, she slipped it from the protective plastic bag and opened it. The title of the fifth installment of the series—"The Secret's Out"—blazed across the top of the page. The article covered everything from how young women no longer felt the need to hide their pregnancy to changes in adoption procedure and how the freedom of information act was making records available for people who wanted to find out about their beginnings.

Since J.R. was still sleeping, Laura poured herself a mug of coffee and sat at the table to read the piece. She was just finishing when the phone rang. She grabbed the cordless and turned it on before the ringing woke J.R.

"Hello."

"Ms. Ramirez?"

"Yes?" Laura frowned. The voice wasn't familiar, yet Laura sensed she'd heard it before.

"This is Regina Barnette. Mrs. Tom Barnette."

"Yes, Mrs. Barnette, I recognize the name," Laura said, her frown deepening. Why on earth was Regina Barnette calling her?

"I apologize for calling you at home, but the man

at the paper said you'd taken the day off, and I found your home number in Tom's Rolodex.''

"I see," Laura said, but she didn't. Not at all.

"I've been keeping up with your adoption series," Regina said. "It's excellent work. Very thorough, and for journalism, very emotional.''

Ah, Laura thought. A fan call.

"Thank you, Mrs. Barnette. I appreciate your taking the time to call.''

"Oh, I'm not calling just to praise you. I'm calling because... Oh, I've been thinking of contacting you ever since Sunday, but after I read today's piece, I decided I couldn't wait any longer. The truth is, I believe I possess some information that might interest your paper and the voters of the state, what with the election coming up and everything.''

Though Laura had no idea where the woman was coming from, Mrs. Barnette had managed to pique her interest. What kind of information could Regina have that she thought would make good copy this close to the election? It must be something that would clear her husband's name and secure his senatorial seat.

"I wasn't sure who to give the information to," Regina said, clearly nervous, "but I decided that since you'd been talking to Tom about Jake Lattimer and that Texas Ranger fellow getting separated, and since you're doing this adoption series, you were the logical one to tell.''

The mention of Jake and Zach threw a kink into Laura's theory about Regina clearing Tom's name. "To tell what, Mrs. Barnette?" she asked, uncertain where their conversation was headed.

Regina Barnette took a deep breath. "My husband

had an affair with our baby-sitter more than thirty-five years ago.''

Baby-sitter. Laura's heart began to pound heavily. Tom had told her or Ben—she couldn't remember—that he'd sent his baby-sitter to stay with Lillian. He'd elected to omit one vital piece of information—that he was the one who'd gotten her pregnant.

"She was a nice girl, or I thought she was," Regina said. "Her daddy was a preacher. When I found out what had happened, I was furious. And hurt."

"Mrs. Barnette, you don't have to tell me this," Laura said, sensitive to the pain in the woman's voice, even though her heart raced with anticipation.

"Oh, yes, my dear, I do," Regina said, and launched into her tale again. "Our girls were small—I married Tom straight out of high school—and I didn't have any skills but typing. I didn't know how I'd make it on my own if I left him, and he promised me it would never happen again."

She laughed. "I was more trusting back then than I am now, and I believed him. So he paid for her to go to that home in Brownsboro and promised her complete secrecy if she'd stay out of our lives. To my knowledge he never talked to her after that. I don't know what happened to her or her child."

Laura's mind reeled with the certainty swirling through it. Tom Barnette was the man Abby had had the affair with, the older man Chip Brownlee had alluded to.

"Mrs. Barnette, do you remember the girl's name? I may know what happened to her baby."

"Of course I do! I'll never forget it. Her name was Abby Pickett."

Laura gasped as the last piece of the puzzle fell

into place. If Tom had fathered Abby's babies and those babies were switched with Jake and Zach at the hospital, that meant Tom Barnette was Logan and Russ's father. Laura's mind whirled. She thought of Lillian Hampstead's lies. This was what she'd been hiding.

The first coherent thought that worked its way through Laura's shock was that Logan would have a coronary. But before she told him what she'd learned, she had to talk to Regina Barnette.

"Mrs. Barnette, I have a story to tell you about your husband. It's long and involved, but I think you should hear it."

"Oh, definitely," Regina said. "Where can I meet you?"

Laura explained that Rufio was sick, and Regina agreed to meet her at home within the hour.

They were about to hang up when Laura asked, "Mrs. Barnette, why have you chosen now to tell all this? Aren't you afraid of ruining your husband's chances of winning the election?"

"That's exactly why I am telling it, my dear," Regina said. "You see, I just found out that my husband is involved in another affair."

Her sarcastic laughter filtered through the phone lines. "She's young and pretty and the latest in a very long line. She called me at my home and asked me to give my husband a divorce, which I've decided to do. But nothing is free, and Tom's going to pay for this divorce—in every way a man can pay. And that, Ms. Ramirez, includes the possibility of losing the election."

She laughed again. "Revenge isn't very nice, but if it's all you have, it'll do."

* * *

"Let me see if I have this right," Regina said when Laura finished her tale. "The boys Jack and Valerie Campbell raised—Logan and Russ—are Tom's sons?"

"That's exactly what I'm saying."

Regina laughed with pure delight. "Oh, that's rich!" she said, wiping her eyes. "Tom's own son is working overtime to ruin him." Sobering, she looked at the ceiling and said, "Yes, Regina, there is a God." Then she asked, "How on earth did this mix-up happen?"

"We aren't sure." Laura explained about the chaos at the hospital the night the two sets of twins were born. "All we know is that they were somehow switched by Lillian Hampstead—"

"Whom Tom also slept with," Regina interjected bitterly.

"Who, according to a couple of sources, may have been involved in selling babies."

"I wouldn't put it past her."

"The person who gave me the information about Lillian believes Tom was part of it, too. What do you think?" Laura asked.

Regina considered the possibility. "I'm not saying he wasn't, but shuffling around numbers on paper and creating fake companies is one thing. Stealing someone's baby and selling it is too...I don't know, too *personal,* for lack of a better word."

She shook her head. "Maybe he was involved, but I can't see it. Whatever else he is, Tom's been a pretty decent father. And he loves his children and his grandchildren."

The words slammed into Laura like an eighteen-wheeler roaring down the interstate. *Madré de Dios!* Why hadn't she realized it sooner?

Tom Barnette was not only Logan and Russ's father—he was J.R.'s grandfather.

The last thing on earth Laura wanted to do was confront Tom Barnette with the information his wife had revealed, but Laura knew that, like it or not, it was something she had to do, and it should be done face-to-face. She wanted to look him in the eye when she told him Logan and Russ were his sons. She wanted to see his reaction when she told him about J.R.

Laura fully expected to be told Tom was out of the office or that he couldn't see her, but to her surprise, he invited her in.

The first time she'd met him, Laura thought he looked familiar. Now she knew why. Tom was still a handsome man, and both his sons had inherited the best of his physical attributes. There was much of Tom in Logan and Russ. She hoped they'd inherited only the best of his other characteristics, as well.

He stood when she entered the room, a polite smile on his face. "Ms. Ramirez. What have you turned up now?"

"Hello, Mr. Barnette," Laura said, thinking that he looked older than the last time she'd seen him. "I've turned up plenty. May I sit down?"

"Surely." He waved her toward a leather chair and sat down across from her.

"There's no use beating around the bush," she said, leaning back and crossing her legs. "I spoke with a woman a few days ago who stayed at Lillian Hampstead's home when she was sixteen. This woman believes that Lillian told her her baby was dead so she could sell it on the black market."

"Lillian? Selling babies? Why on earth would you believe a story like that?" Tom asked with a condescending smile. "I know you've had a lot of unanswered questions about the switch involving Ben's boy and the Campbell twins, but you're grasping at straws here. You told me yourself it was crazy at the hospital that night. As an investigative reporter, you should know that an honest mistake does not a criminal make, Ms. Ramirez."

"The woman involved doesn't think it's farfetched, and she believes she can find others who stayed in Brownsboro who feel the same way. There's at least one former employee who also thinks something illegal was going on. And," she continued, "just to keep the record straight, I don't believe I insinuated there was any wrongdoing in regards to the Campbell-Lattimer situation."

"My mistake," he said, barely concealing his irritation and his sarcasm. "So do you mind telling me what this has to do with me?"

"You and Mrs. Hampstead worked together on several adoptions," she stated.

"That's right," he said with a nod.

"Then my question to you is simple. Were you partners with her in a black-market baby operation?"

His shock seemed genuine.

"No, I was not," he said emphatically. "Look, I know this Aegean Insurance thing has blighted my character, but why on earth would you think I was involved with something like that?"

"Where there's smoke, there's fire."

Tom glared at her. "Not this time."

"I'll take your word for now, but believe me, I intend to dig until I find out the truth."

"You can dig to China and back again, and you won't find anything to link me to black-market adoptions." He started to rise, indicating that their interview was at an end.

"I'm glad to hear that," she said, and found that, whether or not it was the truth, she meant it, for J.R.'s sake. "I need just a few more minutes of your time."

"Make it quick, then," he said, sitting down.

"You told me you trusted Lillian, and that's why you sent your baby-sitter there when she got in trouble and her family came to you for help."

"That's correct."

"What if I told you your wife came to see me this morning and told me that you were the father of that young girl's child—Abby Pickett, wasn't it?"

Watching the color drain from his face was all the proof Laura needed of his culpability. For once in his life, he didn't try to bluster his way out of it. All he said, was, "Dear God, Regina."

"Obviously, it's true." When he made no reply, she said, "Do you ever think about the child Abby gave birth to?"

If possible, Tom's face paled even more. He pulled a handkerchief from his pocket and mopped at his forehead. "What's this all about, Ms. Ramirez? Money? Are you trying to blackmail me?"

Laura laughed, but inside, she felt sick at being the one responsible for bringing everything out in the open. Still, she knew it was important for the truth to be told. No good could come from lies and deceit.

"I have no plans to blackmail you, Mr. Barnette,

or to repeat anything you tell me to the media. All I'm trying to do is find out the truth for a friend.''

"Truth? Why don't you ask Regina? She seems anxious enough to spill her guts,'' he said, his voice dripping sarcasm.

"Regina doesn't have the answers I need. You do.'' She looked at him, searching his eyes as if they might reveal the answers to the secrets he'd held inside so long. "Did Lillian ever tell you if Abby had a girl or boy?''

"No.'' When she pinned him with a probing look, he added, "I figured it was better for all concerned if I didn't know.''

"Didn't you ever wonder?''

"Of course I wondered,'' he told her, his face suffused with a strange combination of anger and regret. "But I never asked. In fact, when Abby went to stay with Lillian I told her that when the child was born, I wanted it placed with a couple who lived as far away from the Dallas area as she could.''

The final piece of the puzzle fell into place. Finally, Laura understood exactly what had happened.

"Abby gave birth to twin boys, Mr. Barnette.''

"Twins?'' Incredulity showed on his face. "Are you serious? Do you know where they are?''

She nodded. "They're in New Orleans.''

"New Orleans? How did they wind up there?''

"You just said it. You told Lillian to get them as far away from Dallas as she could. When Valerie Campbell went into labor and her boys, Jake and Zach, were born the same night as your and Abby's sons, Lillian saw a prime opportunity to do as you asked. All she had to do to make you happy was switch the babies. The situation with the weather, no doctor, all the confusion just made her job that much easier, more believable if the truth ever did come out.''

Laura waited for Tom to think over what she'd said, waited for him to come to the same conclusion she had.

The eyes that met hers were bleak, defeated. ''You said Jake Lattimer and Zach Rawlings are the Campbells' sons.'' Laura nodded. ''If that's true—and I can make Lilli tell me—then that means the boys Jack raised, Logan and Russ Campbell, are mine.''

At his stammered request, Laura started in May with Georgia mistaking Zach for Jake and took Tom through the unfolding of the twins mix-up step by heartbreaking step. Seeing him come to terms with the fact that one of his blood sons wanted nothing more than to see him ruined wasn't easy for Laura, even though she wasn't overly fond of Tom herself.

Nor was it easy to tell him about her relationship with Russ, and that he had a grandson. But she did it. His eyes filled with tears as he stared at Rufio's picture and murmured, ''He looks a lot like my Jennifer's little boy.''

Laura left his office an hour later, uncertain about what Tom would do with the truths he'd learned. It wasn't any of her business. She left him sitting at his desk, his head in his hands—husband, father, grandfather, senatorial candidate, philanderer, possible jailbird, a humble, broken man. She felt no pleasure at bringing him to this point, but she felt strongly that, just as the twins whose lives had been affected did, Tom Barnette deserved to know the truth.

* * *

Feeling pretty broken herself, Laura went home to relieve Inez of her baby-sitting duties. Inez assured Laura that J.R. was back to normal. Laura hugged her sister, thanked her and told her again there were no hard feelings over her forgetfulness the day before.

Laura stood in the doorway and watched her sister back down the driveway through a pouring rain. She rubbed at her throbbing temple. One thing was certain. There was nothing like a new crisis to make a person forget their problems. At least she hadn't spent the morning crying her heart out over Russ.

She went into the kitchen and stared at the cordless phone lying on the countertop as if it were some sort of monster that would bite off her hand the moment she picked it up. She dreaded making the call to Logan but knew that putting it off wouldn't make it any easier.

There was little doubt that his reaction to the news would be explosive. But what would Russ think about being Tom Barnette's son?

Russ, who'd decided he was a glutton for punishment, sat slouched in a chair in Logan's office while his brother used every nuance of his not inconsiderable expertise to persuade Russ to give himself and Laura another chance.

When Logan's secretary announced that he had a call from Ms. Ramirez about the investigation, he said he'd take it and pushed a button that would make his conversation audible to Russ.

He flicked Russ a grin and answered Laura's, "Hi, Logan," with, "I know, I know, my brother is an idiot! Give it a few days. Maybe I can talk some sense into him."

"I hope so," Laura said. The admission caused Russ's heart to give a little leap.

"I didn't call about me and Russ. I called because a source came forward with information about your and Russ's paternity."

Logan's gaze found Russ's. He arched his eyebrows. "Oh?"

Russ heard a wary, cautious note in his brother's voice and knew he was being bombarded by doubts and second thoughts, as Russ was. It was one thing to think you wanted to know the truth about something, another to stand face to face with that truth.

"Is the source reliable?" Logan asked, his gaze clinging to Russ's, as if he needed some contact, some means of emotional support.

"I'd say so. It's the man's wife."

Logan blew out a harsh breath. Russ's breathing stopped.

"I'd say that's reliable enough." Logan tugged at the tie knotted at his throat. "Give it to me straight."

"You aren't going to like it."

"The only thing I positively, absolutely couldn't take is if you told me my old man is Tom Barnette," Logan quipped with dry sarcasm.

For a second or two, Laura didn't answer. A strange and horrible premonition descended over Russ. A nervous laugh came through the phone lines and he heard her say, "He is."

Shock reverberated through Russ, leaving him feeling stunned and fragmented as questions with no answers and half-formed thoughts tumbled through his mind.

Logan hooted with laughter. "That's a good one,

Laura, but I never took you for the kind of woman who had a vicious streak.''

"Logan." Her voice sounded tired, filled with extreme patience. "I'm not being vicious."

The smile slid from Logan's face like hot butter off a stack of pancakes.

When he didn't reply, she said, "Listen to me carefully. I'm not joking. I have this straight from Regina Barnette's mouth. Tom Barnette is your father."

Laura spent the next few minutes explaining things to Logan. She told him that Abby had been the Barnettes' baby-sitter when Tom seduced her, and that he'd sent her to stay with Lillian at the Brownsboro home, getting her away from the public eye in return for her silence. She revealed how Tom had told Lillian to get Abby's baby as far away from him and his family as possible.

Always quick on the uptake, Logan said, "That's why she switched us, isn't it?"

"I think so."

Logan swore. "I'll send that biddy to prison for the rest of her life if it's the last thing I do."

"I'm no lawyer, Logan, but I think it will be hard to make anyone believe she did it on purpose. It's her word against Tom's. He's already in hot water, and I'm not sure anyone would believe him these days. Lillian is a fragile-looking little thing with a sweet smile and this charming, gee-it-was-so-long-ago-I-can't-remember way about her, which, I might add, is nothing but some Oscar-worthy acting. Add that to what we already know about the situation at the hospital that night, and there isn't a jury in the state that would find her guilty."

"It's worth a try."

"What would it change?"

Laura's heart stumbled, then began to race. The simple question had been voiced by Russ. She didn't know he'd been in the room with Logan all this time.

"It would make me feel better," Logan said.

"Would it?" Russ responded. "Tom Barnette would still be our father. If you hate that idea so much, why would you want to make it public knowledge, drag out all the dirt for everyone to drool over? Is it worth putting Mom—all of us—through that just to get to Barnette?"

Laura could picture the expressions on their faces as she listened to the short exchange.

"No," Logan said at last. "I guess not. But he should pay."

"He is," Laura said. "His wife is leaving him. And whether you believe it or not, he's pretty torn up about this."

"So we let Lillian go scott-free?"

"Maybe not." Laura told them about Barbara Cauthon's allegations and Ruthie Parker's feelings that Barbara was telling the truth, adding, "All I need is some proof, and I'm determined to look until I find it."

Logan's laughter was short but filled with admiration. "Well, I, for one, have no doubts you'll do it."

Laura got off the phone soon afterward and made her way into the kitchen. Logan had responded to the news about Tom just as she'd expected. Surprisingly, Russ, usually the hothead, seemed to be more philosophical about Tom Barnette's past and future influence in their lives.

She fixed a pot of coffee, needing the caffeine to

keep her awake and the warmth to drive away the chill of the rainy afternoon and the wintry feeling that swept through her whenever she thought of Russ.

Don't think of him.

Easier said than done. She sat at the table and rested her head in her hands. Logan's assurances that she could bring Lillian to justice ran through her head. How could she prove Lillian Hampstead had been stealing and selling babies? Maybe she should leave it alone and send Barbara and her suspicions to the police.

As if they don't have enough to do without trying to prove a thirty-year-old crime.

All right, then, maybe Zach and Shelby could give her some idea about how to proceed, where to look.

Not today, Laura.

No, not today. Her emotions felt as if they'd been through the wringer, or maybe the shredder.

"Mom?"

She looked up and saw J.R. standing in the doorway. "Yeah, *niño?*"

"Why did Russ go back to New Orleans without saying goodbye?"

A sliver of pain worked its way into her heart. "I don't know, Rufio. Maybe he had some business to take care of."

"Yeah. Maybe. Is he going to call tonight? I need to tell him I'm okay. He was real worried about me."

Laura clamped her teeth on her bottom lip to still its sudden trembling. "I don't know. Hey," she said, forcing a smile and hoping to change the subject, "how about a cup of hot cocoa?"

"No, thanks," he said, his eyes grave as he turned started down the hall.

Laura watched him go, her heart aching. Then, exhausted physically and mentally, she put her head on her folded arms and wept out her misery to the empty room.

From the hallway, J.R. listened, frowning.

Laura's mood deteriorated on Friday. So did J.R.'s. By Saturday, out of sorts because Russ hadn't called, he pouted or cried about everything. Laura retaliated by snapping at him over the slightest thing—which only made her feel worse, because she knew the fault was more hers than his. Hers and Russ's.

When J.R. went down for a nap on Saturday afternoon, she went to bed and indulged in another bout of crying.

J.R. heard, and with his heart pounding fast in his chest, he let himself into her room, crawled onto the bed and whispered, "What's wrong, Mom?"

Her hand was pressed against her heart, and she tried to smile. "I'm just sad, Rufio."

He put his hand over hers. "Missing Russ makes me hurt, too."

The words made more tears run down her cheeks. J.R. was glad when she pulled him beside her. It made him feel better to be close to her. He hoped it made her feel better, too. He lay there until she fell asleep, then went into the living room where the phone had people's numbers programmed into it.

Zach Rawlings was watching college football on television when the phone rang. "I'll get it!" he called to Georgia, who was in the kitchen fixing dinner.

He picked up the cordless phone. "Rawlings."

"Zach?" The voice belonged to a child.

"J.R.?"

"Yes, sir."

"Are you okay?" All Zach's cop instincts told him something wasn't right. "Where's your mother?"

"Asleep. Zach, do you know how to get hold of Russ? I don't have his number in New Orleans, but I really need to talk to him."

"J.R., is everything okay? Is your mom okay?"

"We're fine," he said, then sighed and added, "well, not so good, really. Mom's crying a lot because she misses Russ, and I really need to talk to him."

J.R. sounded close to tears himself. Zach didn't know what had happened, but he'd darn well see that J.R. talked to Russ.

"I don't have his number, pardner, but I'll get it and give you a call back, okay?"

"Okay."

J.R. sat on the sofa, the phone in his lap, staring at a landscape picture hanging on the wall and waiting for Zach to call back.

When the phone rang, he grabbed it on the first ring so it wouldn't wake his mom. "Hello?"

"J.R., this is Russ. Zach said I should call you."

Relief gushed through J.R. He felt the tears he wouldn't cry in front of Zach fill his eyes.

"Dad," he said, his voice breaking over a sob. "You've gotta come quick. It's Mom."

"Laura? What's wrong with her?"

"She's crying. She said her heart is hurting. She misses you."

There was a long pause. J.R. was beginning to

wonder if his dad was still there when he said, "Hold the fort, kiddo. I'm on my way."

When Laura woke from her nap almost an hour later, her nose was stuffy and she felt strangely empty from her crying. She found Rufio in the living room. He was on his knees in one of the overstuffed chairs, his arms resting across the back, looking out the window at the pelting rain. She decided to leave him alone with his thoughts, whatever they were. She wasn't up to trying to explain why Russ had suddenly exited their lives.

Fifteen minutes later, he was still ensconced in the chair. "Are you expecting someone?" she teased, determined to alter her attitude and her mood.

"Dad," he said, not bothering to turn around.

Laura's heart ached. It was the first time she'd ever heard J.R. refer to Russ as Dad. *"Niño,"* she said gently. "Russ isn't coming."

J.R. turned to look at her over his shoulder. "Yes, he is. He said he was."

"What? When?"

"I called him," J.R. announced proudly. "Well, not Russ. I didn't know his number, but I called Zach, and he had Russ call me."

Horrified, but nonetheless impressed by J.R.'s initiative, Laura said, "Your dad called while I was asleep?"

J.R. nodded. "I told him you were sad and you missed him."

"Oh, Rufio!"

"It's true, isn't it? You say I should always tell the truth."

"Yes, but..." Laura stopped. There was no use

discussing the finer points of heartache to a five-year-old. Instead, she went to him and, leaning over, gave him a hug. "Come on. I'm hungry. Let's fix a sandwich or something."

"I have to wait for Dad."

As if on cue, the gleam of headlights slashed through the rainy night into the room.

"There he is!"

"That can't be your dad. Even if he does come, he won't be here any time soon. He's in New Orleans, remember?"

Shrugging off her hold and her words, J.R. leaped off the chair and hurtled through the doorway into the small foyer. Laura followed. Whoever was at the door, J.R. shouldn't answer it alone, not after dark.

She reached the entryway as J.R. clicked the dead bolt and swung the door open. Russ stood there, wearing a long-sleeve knit shirt of forest green, his russet hair sprinkled with raindrops that glittered in the overhead light.

Her eyes met his. She couldn't tell what he was feeling, but she felt an intense relief that he'd come. He looked so big and strong and dependable that she wanted nothing more than to let him wrap those muscular arms around her and hold her forever.

J.R. turned to Laura, a wide grin on his face. "I told you."

"Yes," she said. "You did."

J.R. reached out and took Russ's hand in his. His fingers swallowed Rufio's.

"Don't be mad at me, Dad," he said, his voice cracking. "I didn't mean to get sick."

A spasm of pain crossed Russ's features. Still holding Rufio's hand, he squatted so he could look into the boy's eyes. "I'm not mad at you, J.R. I'm mad at myself. I pushed you too hard."

"No, you didn't!" J.R. denied. "I'm tough. I can take it. I want to get good at baseball."

"You will," Russ said. "You can't expect to do it perfect in a few days. It takes time and practice."

"I'll work hard," J.R. said. "Every day, if…if you stay here and be my dad for real. Will you?"

Laura saw Russ's Adam's apple move as if he were swallowing an obstruction, then he scooped Rufio into his arms and stood. Rufio put his arms around Russ's neck. "Please."

"That's up to your mom," Russ said, his gaze finding Laura's. "I'm not sure I'll make a good husband. And I don't think I've done a very good job of being a dad."

Laura saw the love and uncertainty in his eyes. Her love filled her heart to almost bursting. It wouldn't be easy living with Russ Campbell, but then she'd probably go crazy with boredom if her life ever got too simple.

"You can't expect to do it perfect in a few days," she said, crossing to where they stood. "It takes time and practice."

"Yeah!" J.R. said, smiling. "If you're tough and you work hard, you can do it."

"You think so?" Russ asked, sliding an arm around Laura's shoulders and pulling her against him.

"I know so," she told him, and lifted her lips for his kiss.

Epilogue

Times-Picayune, December 25

Joanna Bliss Abernathy and John Logan Campbell, both of New Orleans, were married at four o'clock yesterday evening at the St. Michael's Church, in what will be remembered as the wedding of the year for years to come. The Christmas bride was drop-dead gorgeous in a long-sleeve Jessica McClintock gown of winter white velvet. Ms. Abernathy's intricately coiffed hair was wound through with pearls and white camellias, which were echoed in her bouquet of white rosebuds and holly.

Flaunting tradition, Ms. Abernathy's wedding party consisted entirely of married friends. Mrs. Zachery Rawlings of Fort Worth and Mrs. Jacob Lattimer of Aledo, Texas, wore unadorned gowns of forest green velvet and carried tussie mussies of holly and ivy. Matron of honor was her sister-in-law, popular Dallas television journalist Laura Campbell.

James Russell Campbell, the groom's brother, served as best man. Groomsmen were Zachery Rawlings, Jacob Lattimer and Elliot "Buzz" Abernathy, the bride's business partner.

Miss Leza Perez, daughter of Rosalita and Ernesto Perez of Aledo, was Ms. Abernathy's flower girl, and Master James Russell Campbell, nephew of the bride and groom, served as ring bearer.

The New Orleans country club was a winter wonderland of white poinsettias and fresh evergreen boughs threaded with strands of pearls, and white, silver and gold lamé ribbon.

A string quartet served background music while the wedding guests—some two hundred of them—mingled and chatted while sipping on champagne and nibbling on shrimp and caviar, which, along with a smorgasbord of other culinary delicacies, surrounded an ice sculpture of Botticelli's Venus as she rose from the sea.

The groom's mother, former wife of "Black Jack" Campbell, was escorted by Texas cattleman Mr. Benjamin Lattimer, also of Aledo. In an unexpected surprise, Mrs. Campbell and Mr. Lattimer announced their own engagement at the reception.

Tom Barnette, who'd stood on the fringes of the crowd outside the church hoping to catch at least a glimpse of his son and his bride, skimmed the account of Logan's wedding with a feeling of sick regret.

He'd tried on more than one occasion to talk to Logan, but his eldest son refused to grant him even five minutes.

Undaunted, and encouraged by a meeting with Russ, Tom's daughters, Jennifer and Stephanie, planned to call Logan after the first of the year to see if there was any chance to forge at least a casual friendship. Tom hoped it worked out for them.

Through Laura's urging, Tom had met Russ and J.R., and while he didn't hold out much hope for ever having more than a cursory relationship with them, Russ was at least civil, which was more than could be said of most people. Since he'd lost the election, Regina had left him, and he'd been indicted in the Aegean Insurance case.

Tom was out on bail until the trial, which was set for mid-spring. His attorney, who felt his actions and involvement were only borderline illegal, thought he had a good chance of getting out of the mess without serving any hard time.

Only Tom knew that was a sentence he was already serving.

Even Ashlie had abandoned him, saying that the negative press was bad for her acting career. The last he'd heard, the only thing she was pursuing was a Dallas Cowboy football player who'd just signed a multimillion-dollar five-year contract.

The good news was that Tom had been absolved of any wrongdoing in connection to the black-market baby case brought against Lillian Hampstead. That story had broken the day following Laura and Russ's reconciliation when Lillian's cousin, Ruthie Parker, checked her flooded garage and saw that some boxes Lillian had stored there when she'd moved from Brownsboro several years before had gotten soaked.

Worried about damage to the contents, she'd opened the boxes and found, to her horror, years of paperwork detailing Lillian's involvement in selling babies to wealthy families. Tom still had a hard time believing Lilli was capable of such atrocities, but he'd seen in the Dallas paper that she would be going to trial soon after the first of the year. He should have realized sooner that she was guilty of wrong-doing. Once Laura Ramirez had told him about the switch, a fragment of conversation he'd had with Lillian had once come back to him. She'd actually used the word switched, instead of separated when he'd talked to her about Jake and Zach.

He folded the paper and laid it on the nightstand, wondering which restaurant he might go to for Christmas dinner where he wouldn't be recognized. Regina was spending the day with the girls, which meant they couldn't ask him to join the family festivities.

Merry Christmas, Barnette.

The phone rang. Tom snatched it up, his eagerness a testimony to his loneliness. "Hello."

"Dad? This is Jennifer."

"Jen?" he said, feeling near tears. "Merry Christmas."

"Merry Christmas to you, too. Hold on. Mom wants to talk to you."

There was the sound of the receiver changing hands and then Tom heard Regina say, "Tom?"

"Merry Christmas, Regina." Tom heard the humility and the thickness of tears in his voice. He didn't care. The truth was, he missed her.

"Don't read more into this than there is, but it's Christmas, and the girls would like you to come over and have dinner with us."

"What about you, Gina?"

He heard her sigh. "I never was one to hold a grudge for long." She sighed again. "The truth is, I can't bear to think of you sitting in that empty apartment alone on Christmas."

"You always did have a big heart, Gina," he said with a wistful, regretful smile.

"For all the good it did me."

"No," he said, "for all the good it did me."

Regina didn't speak for several seconds, and when she did, it was to give him the time for dinner, adding, "Don't be late."

Assuring her that he wouldn't, Tom hung up and headed for the shower, his heart lighter than it had been in weeks. Things were looking up. Whatever happened in court, his family hadn't completely turned its back on him. He was having Christmas dinner with his girls.

The new year was a week away. A new year, a time to regroup, to rethink, to plan for the future and make restitution for the mistakes of the past.

Spring, a time of rebirth and renewal, would soon follow. Maybe, he thought, as a kernel of hope sprouted inside him, he could find a way to win back his wife and bridge the chasm that separated him from his sons.

* * * * *

Return to the Towers!

In March
New York Times bestselling author

NORA ROBERTS

brings us to the Calhouns' fabulous
Maine coast mansion and reveals the
tragic secrets hidden there for generations.

For all his degrees, Professor Max Quartermain has a
lot to learn about love—and luscious Lilah Calhoun is
just the woman to teach him. Ex-cop Holt Bradford is
as prickly as a thornbush—until Suzanna Calhoun's
special touch makes love blossom in his heart.
And all of them are caught in the race to solve
the generations-old mystery of a priceless
lost necklace...and a timeless love.

Lilah and Suzanna
THE
Calhoun Women

**A special 2-in-1 edition containing
FOR THE LOVE OF LILAH and
SUZANNA'S SURRENDER**

Available at your favorite retail outlet.

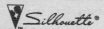

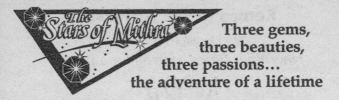

The Stars of Mithra

Three gems,
three beauties,
three passions...
the adventure of a lifetime

SILHOUETTE·INTIMATE·MOMENTS®
brings you a thrilling new series by
New York Times bestselling author

Nora Roberts

Three mystical blue diamonds place three close
friends in jeopardy...and lead them to romance.

In October
HIDDEN STAR (IM#811)
Bailey James can't remember a thing, but she knows
she's in big trouble. And she desperately needs private
investigator Cade Parris to help her live long enough to
find out just what kind.

In December
CAPTIVE STAR (IM#823)
Cynical bounty hunter Jack Dakota and spitfire
M. J. O'Leary are handcuffed together and on the run
from a pair of hired killers. And Jack wants to know
why—but M.J.'s not talking.

In February
SECRET STAR (IM#835)
Lieutenant Seth Buchanan's murder investigation takes
a strange turn when Grace Fontaine turns up alive. But
as the mystery unfolds, he soon discovers the notorious
heiress is the biggest mystery of all.

Available at your favorite retail outlet.

**Make a Valentine's date
for the premiere of**

◈ HARLEQUIN® **Movies**

starting February 14, 1998 with

Debbie Macomber's
This Matter of
Marriage

on

Just tune in to **The Movie Channel** the **second Saturday
night** of every month at 9:00 p.m. EST to join us, and be swept
away by the sheer thrill of romance brought to life. Watch for
details of upcoming movies—in books, in your television
viewing guide and in stores.

If you are not currently a subscriber to The Movie Channel,
simply call your local cable or satellite provider for more
details. Call today, and don't miss out on the romance!

**100% pure movies.
100% pure fun.**

Makes any time special.™

An Alliance Production

HMBPA298

SANDRA STEFFEN

**Continues the
twelve-book series—
36 Hours—in February 1998
with Book Eight**

MARRIAGE BY CONTRACT

Nurse Bethany Kent could think of only one man who could make her dream come true: Dr. Tony Petrocelli, the man who had helped her save the life of the infant she desperately wanted to adopt. As husband and wife, they could provide the abandoned baby with a loving home. But could they provide each other with more than just a convenient marriage?

For Tony and Bethany and *all* the residents of Grand Springs, Colorado, the storm-induced blackout was just the beginning of 36 Hours that changed *everything!* You won't want to miss a single book.

Available at your favorite retail outlet.

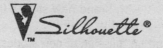

DIANA PALMER
ANN MAJOR
SUSAN MALLERY

MONTANA MAVERICKS *Weddings*

RETURN TO WHITEHORN

In **April 1998** get ready to catch the bouquet. Join in the excitement as these bestselling authors lead us down the aisle with three heartwarming tales of love and matrimony in Big Sky country.

A very engaged lady is having second thoughts about her intended; a pregnant librarian is wooed by the town bad boy; a cowgirl meets up with her first love. Which Maverick will be the next one to get hitched?

Available in **April 1998.**

Silhouette's beloved **MONTANA MAVERICKS** returns in Special Edition and Harlequin Historicals starting in February 1998, with brand-new stories from your favorite authors.

Round up these great new stories at your favorite retail outlet.

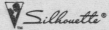

PSMMWEDS